The Rose Room

June Moore

ISBN:1519722281
ISBN-13:9781519722287

DEDICATION

With grateful thanks to Shirley and all my friends at
Baildon Scribblers for their advice and support.

ACKNOWLEDGMENTS

Cover by Anne Carr, Yorkshire Artist

JUNE D. MOORE'S OTHER BOOKS on KINDLE:

<u>THE RIVER SERIES:</u>

'WILD RIVER'

'RIVER REVENGE'

.

CHAPTER ONE

During one particular hard winter an event occurred which was destined to drag the village of Elvingdale onto the front pages of the tabloid newspapers.

The weather had been turbulent with heavy snows. Wild winds had turned a million flakes into unfamiliar walls as a hearse wound its way down the drive from 'The Croft', the Dales' stone house where Emily Gatenby had spent her life; a single black hearse, no followers. White hills and tall overburdened trees made a sombre if impressive backdrop. The wheels crunched on a fresh powdery covering where previous blizzard conditions had swept the drive almost bare. One forlorn spray of flowers sat on the coffin inside.

Genna had watched from high ground not far away. The dog beside her sat with alert, pricked ears perhaps anticipating a job to be done. The village had been cut off with the drifts of the last few days but that had little to do with the lack of mourners at Emily Gatenby's funeral; Genna knew about that.

The dark shape had continued down into the lane overhung with crystal branches; a gracious archway for the departure of its occupant. Slowly it crept like a large black slug, past the old rectory to the church on the outskirts of the village and disappeared from the view of its observers.

The journey of an old reclusive spinster as she left

her solitary domain for the final time, could certainly not have any particular dramatic or far reaching significance for a young girl like herself. She dismissed the thought.

"Genna, there was a call for you while you were sorting the washing." Genna turned with the pile of damp clothes in her arms. Who could be ringing her this early in the morning? Who would ever be phoning her these days? She had no admirers in the village. Work had got around she was too busy and not on the market. Her mother was calling again.

"Can you ring back later today, she's left a mobile number for you."

"Who, Mum, for heaven's sake, who?"

"ISSY, of course… says she's got big news."

Genna shivered as she hung the damp, heavy clothes on the line. Her fingers were going numb with the morning cold. She turned away from clean but grey, worn looking underwear belonging to herself and her mother. Her gaze shifted to the frost covered fields and their webs of stone boundaries. The land disappeared dipping away suddenly and steeply into a hidden valley only to reappear up the other side of the dale, a craggy green wall shimmering with ice in the early sun.

She marvelled at the view as she had done many times since being a small child. Somehow views made her tingle. It was a sight that people travelled from all around to enjoy. Tired with the

2

harassment of city streets, exhaust fumes and stress, they inhaled lungs full of clean, green air and surveyed the scenery for a day, or holidayed for longer. A sheep disturbed the silence from across the valley bleating at some difficulty in its life.

Genna struggles with a broken peg and a T shirt, reminding herself to sew up the hole where she had snagged it on barbed wire. She though for the umpteenth time how extraordinary it would be to have really new clothes, white knickers.

Farming was on the skids with Foot and Mouth disease, not to mention the meagre price for lambs. Her father was trying to ignore the fact. But she was committed to help and she would - just get on with it.

School had been different; friends were many and learning was easy, but friends had left to earn money for mobiles, megabytes, DVDS, real knicker buying money.

She remembered the love stories she had read that had fascinated her the most in her early teens. Some Lochinvar from the past would grab the heroine's hand, whisper in her ear and whisk her away from under the nose of a dull adoring swain. She would forget everything, following him into the sunset to share his life and his bed. But these characters were not in her life, no Lord Lochinvar to whip her away, however much she wished there were.

As her contemporaries went on to bigger and

better ways of life, the worst thing had been the dull realisation that her life was not going to expand like theirs, or her mind grow in knowledge other than what she could do for herself, or with a big university debt.

Had her further education become a reality it would have deprived her father of her vital help and strength on the farm, cheap labour maybe. She did not hate him for it, his love of farming the land was a pure thing, she loved him for it and he was good to her. She missed her friends and most of all she missed Issy Farrington. Soon she was going to find out what had happened to her chaotic friend. After months of absence here she was out of the blue with big news.

"Issy?" Genna had found the number with mounting curiosity. What on earth had Issy done now? She had always had a wild impetuous streak at school. She had often turned to Genna's calm sensibility for confirmation, or not, of her actions, even though Genna was younger. "Issy, what's happened?" Where have you been all this time?"

"Genna it's great to talk to you at last. It'll take hours to get up to speed with it all...oh coffee, thanks, Jane. There is actually a lull in this damn department. We never have time to kiss the cat and walk around the table... but it's going to be different."

Genna chortled quietly. Issy hadn't changed. "Go on then tell me, I'm gagging with curiosity."

"Remember Steve, the one I was so daft about?"

"Issy, you're not going to tell me...?"

"Not bloody likely! Steve turned out to be the biggest double dyed rattle snake ever."

"Colourful but deadly?" Genna asked dryly.

"The very same."

"But you escaped in time?"

"I'm escaping now. I'm coming home."

"HOME! But I thought Leeds was a great teaching hospital, really go ahead."

"I've boxed myself into a corner with a dog. When Steve dumped me... yes, he did dump me for somebody else..." Genna heard a pause and Issy gulping, taking a deep breath, "There was this gorgeous puppy, a brindle and white Boxer bitch - last of the litter. I knew she was lonely - just like I felt. She was aching to be loved. I cuddled her and cried - all I did was cry and she licked the tears as though she knew. Anyway mother phoned and I told her about how Fifi was a problem."

"Fifi! What a name for a Boxer puppy!"

"You'll just love her, Genna, anyway mother said father had heard they were advertising for radiographers at Kettlington A. &E. and why didn't I come home for a bit and she would help with Fifi; she's getting bigger, Genna, and she needs to go out more."

Genna remembered all too well how impractical Issy could be, always working on impulse and going for what she wanted with little thought for how it would work.

"The bottom line is, I've been offered a job and I'm home next week...but I wanted to ask you, Gen...could you help? Y'now, I'll be lost and you were always such a rock."

Genna laughed in reply, delighted that life could be about to take an upturn with Issy back and forgetting about how thoughtless her friend could be. "Sure thing, Issy."

Elvingdale was not a large Dales village but it had a distinct and compelling appeal. The cobbled streets with its ancient stone cross were umbrellared with kindly old trees. Here there was an atmosphere of peace, the escape from the world, a Shangri La so beloved by stressed townies.

On the other hand the quaint tea rooms, Dickensian shops and cottages around the edge of the square gave off an enticing hustle and bustle, as though a secret way of life flowed below the surface and was hiding from visitors. Many imagined they could enjoy such a way of life, even bought week-end homes to prove it. Few were really suited and complained about the crowing of early morning roosters and the smell of muck spreading.

Working behind the bar some evenings at the pub, Genna could not help overhearing conversations and at the time it had been easy to discover more about old Emily Gatenby's demise.

"Geoff Cordingly let on as how she'd not take his milk off doorstep for well nigh a week. Dr.

Farrington went in with young bobby. There she wa' in bed, dead as a door stop."

"No sign of that bloody noisy dog?"

"Dead as her. Shut in t'car. Smelt enough to blow roof off. Mind you it wert an old 'un."

"Car?"

"No - y'daft bugger - dog!"

Genna had smiled ruthfully to herself at the flinty attitudes of the longer livers of Elvingdale. She knew Issy's father to be a solid grey haired doctor, not old for his early fifties, one who had the trust and respect of the villagers and his other patients scattered in the more isolated Dale's areas.

Another piece of gossip of late had interested her even more; Issy's brother, now qualified in medicine, had worked at a Leeds hospital, but was about to leave and join his father's practice temporarily or otherwise. Her emotions had soared at the prospect of seeing William again.

The memory of the deep crush she had harboured for William Farrington in her young teens was very clear and she could feel herself colouring all over again at the thought of how, when invited to tea at Issy's, she had dropped her plate along with its cake. She had been so mesmerised at the time with the things William had to say and the interesting way he had of saying them, crumbs had showered all over and she was left covered in cake and embarrassment.

She remembered how she used to dream about him; he would be there before her, gloriously blond and tanned ready to swim, daring her to jump into the deep end of some swimming pool, as perhaps he had done in the distant past. In the dream she had jumped and he had caught her in his arms as she surfaced and kissed her as they disappeared under water. She had felt his hardness against her softness with a feeling of elation she had never know before. She had awakened with wild longings, hoping quickly to go back to sleep to catch up with the dream. Now she may come across him again and be able to see how he had changed, although it was unlikely he would remember her except as a clumsy teenager.

Miss Emily Gatenby
Diary. Summer, 1936.

Visit from Rory and Tom.
They are coming to visit this weekend and will probably stay for a whole week. I cannot sit still. Perhaps I will ask Marion to wave my hair in the way she does for mother, to make me look more grown up and I can wear my dress with the little blue flowers. I think it catches the colour of my eyes.

When I think about Rory I go sort of funny inside and I tingle with expectation at the very thought of being near him, I remember the way he looked at me and those hazel eyes with the dark lashes. Somehow his cheeks are a lovely golden colour like a biscuit but when he smiles there are crinkles around his eyes and mouth. Mother says I must not stare at him so, like the last time, or he will think me rude. I must remember not to.

I must sit quietly and listen to all they have to say and not try to sound clever as mother hates me to. Maybe we will take the horses out. I will not disgrace myself there because I can ride well.

The weather is glorious and we may go down to the river and swim. Pray to God I don't get this wretched blood thing, it is so disgusting. Mother always said she would tell me more about it and it is not a disease as I thought. I won't die, but she always seems reluctant to talk about it properly. I am not scared any more just ashamed about it ever happening.

Father's chest is bad again. I do wish it would get better. Marion says it could be something grassy that is making him breathe badly and is not just the gas that affected his lungs in the last war.

Genna found a parking space near the square. It was early and the tourists would not be around until much later in the morning. Now spring was arriving they would soon snarl up the traffic. She parked the rickety truck and headed for the post office.

Outside the most impressive of the village tea rooms, a figure of uncertain age in overalls and a headscarf, paint brush in one hand, turned to greet her from the top of a ladder.

"Mornin' Genna." The ladder gave an uncertain

lurch,

"Good heavens, Bessie, look out...! It's not safe on those cobbles, it's wobbling all over. I'll hold it so you can climb down."

Bessie seeing the sense of this, turned back carefully as the ladder slithered across the cobblestones swaying precariously. Genna hung on while its occupant gave a series of whoos... and ahhs trying to keep her footing.

Down to the safety of solid ground, the older woman turned and gave Genna's shoulders a quick squeeze. "Bless your lovely blue eyes, darlin' but I've got to do this to be ready for the summer rush. The weather'll bring them out like flies and blisters if it stays the weekend. Best be looking good to take their money."

"Bess, you may as well try a trapeze act while you're up there." Genna knew Bess would like that idea. "Better still ask young Rodney to hold the ladder for you."

Bessie grinned back. "Suppose I should if I could find him. ...bye the way, have you seen the new estate agent over the road".

"At Summers and Goldthorpe?"

"New manager ... an absolute dish. Like the young 'uns say - sex on a stick - that's him."

"I'll keep my eyes peeled. He may come into the pub."

"And what about Issy? Nice for you to have your old friend back. The Farringtons must be pleased about the news. Issy was such a live wire."

Genna marvelled at how quickly news spread through the small village. She heard

Bessie sighed momentarily. Genna understood the sigh, knowing that Bess had lost a little girl with meningitis who would now have been the same age as Issy. "Tell you what, Bess, I hear as how your Roders is turning into something of a babe magnet. How does it feel to have such a gorgeous young guy for a son?" Genna put back the positive slant.

"Terrific! I love him to bits... thank God for him every day. I'll go find him now to hold this damn ladder."

Genna continued her passage to the Post Office uninterrupted, which was quite unusual as she knew so many of the villagers and enjoyed the snippets of local news they usually had to offer. For the first time in months she felt optimistic, spring was on the way, the farm's increasing poverty was pushed into the background and her crazy friend Issy was coming home, dog and all, not to mention a couple of interesting men likely to appear over the horizon.

CHAPTER TWO

The countryside of the Dales is varied, sweeping contours of land snaked with ancient stone walls, limestone pavements, craggy towering cliffs against the sky above, giving an almost tangible feeling of space and visual delight. The sheep inhabiting the place are scraggy creatures under their grey wool, not pretty but tough, being exposed to the harsh climate of the exposed fells.

The eye of the visitor does not see the poverty amongst the farmers and village traders, worse since the foot and mouth outbreak with its closed footpaths and no tourists at the turn of the century.

The wheels put into motion to find the relatives of Emily Gatenby had produced nothing over the past twelve months, for which time the house had stood empty, stripped of its furniture. The advert by solicitors locally and nationally had drawn blanks. She had been a recluse for the latter part of her life and the one floral offering had been sent by her nearest neighbours, Dr. and Mrs. Farrington; flowers sent to show good will, or guilt that they had not managed to befriend a lonely old woman?

'The Rectory' had for the past two decades housed the Farrington family. The practice had originally functioned from the house, but now surgeries were held in a mews property in Elvingdale Village centre. The village had been left in no doubt about the doctor and his wife feeling guilty their old neighbour had been left to die alone. Although they had tried in the past to befriend her, she would have none of it.

Her house. 'The Croft,' under the increasing slope of the hillside and backed by tall sentinel elms, looked down onto woodland and a stream near the boundary of 'The Rectory' land below. The ground was rough and soggy in parts but it was the stream itself which proved to be the next problem in an extraordinary chain of events.

Genna shifted the telephone to her other ear as she switched muddy potatoes round in the bowel before peeling them. "It must be great having William at home. The news soon went round the village about his joining your father's practice."

"Oh sure. He goes out wearing one blue sock and one grey one. He's a clever guy but sometimes you have to knock to get in... well, I do anyway. As a G.P. he'll be first rate."

"I'm surprised he's not married by now." Genna fished.

"He has this la-di-da airhostess called Debora. He met her on holiday last year and fell madly in love. I'll tell you about it when we meet. Mind you, even as a houseman dating nurses he used to choose quite useless specimens. This one's quite removed from normal flesh and blood."

Genna felt some vital energy wane inside her. How stupid! Had she really imagined William was just waiting for her to stroll into his life? Issy was still talking. She pushed the mane of almost black, wavy hair away from her face and fished out another potato.

"His big grouse at the moment is the effect the weather's had on the stream, all the rain, remember it floods the drive from 'The Croft' woods'? It's like a mill race at present. William's car got stuck where it washed away the drive and he came in soaked. Debora is coming next weekend and he wants something done about it. Tell you all about that too. I'll be there at eight, OK?"

"Sorry, Issy, we could be really busy by then. It'll have to be sixish; that should be quieter with all this rain. We can have an in depth natter. I'm so looking forward to it."

Issy would have to fit in for once and Genna put down the phone and went to find her Wellingtons, grabbing an old Mackintosh from behind the door on the way.

She had promised her mother she would clean out the chickens. A fox had been on the prowl lately making it necessary for the hens to be securely shut up at night, or they could face the prospect of dead, bloody and scattered bodies the next morning. The animal rights should take a peep at that sort of scene, they may change their minds about molly coddling what people saw as pretty foxes.

Emily Gatenby, 1937.
Diary notes.

I cannot believe how long it is since last summer and Rory and Tom came to stay. This time it was quite different. I have grown up a lot since then. I suppose it is to do with being sent to boarding school. Having a governess was all very well, father said but I needed finishing off. Most of being finished off is absolutely awful. I cannot be alone when I like, read when I want to, or read what I want. There is very little privacy and some time I have to get undressed and wash in front of other girls. I am shocked at the shapes and sizes of their bodies and how little they seem to care about displaying them.

I suppose on the other hand there are things I have learned (nothing to do with school work) that I needed to know, things which mother in her diffidence would never have told me.

When the boys came this summer I almost knew what to expect. They have grown up too. They told me all about how they are learning to fly and how it was the most exciting thing ever invented.

When we went riding, Tom, who is the younger and only a year older than me, waited when we had been cantering and Rory had gone ahead. He is more boisterous than Rory and sometimes teases me. He told me, 'You used to be plain and now somehow you're not. If you go on like this I shall fall in love with you.' I smiled knowing he was only half serious.

A day or so later Rory and I walked to the bottom of the wood. It was so lovely with the sunshine

sprinkling light and warmth through the trees.
Near the stream there is a big rock where we sat
down. He put his arm around my shoulders in a sort
of casual, friendly way and went on talking. It felt
sensational but then, with his fingers on my chin, he
turned my face to his and kissed me, so gently. I
could not believe it happened. It was glorious. I
knew I had to shut my eyes but my heart was
pounding so fast I could hardly breathe. It goes to
show, telling is one thing, doing is another.

He made me promise mother would never find
out. She would be furious because I was too young
for that sort of thing, even if I did not look it. He
need not have worried, I would never have told
mother anyway. Mother is a remote creature
inhabiting a different world sometimes. I suppose I
am not a lot better but I escape into books. I'm not
sure where she escapes to.

From its spot at the top of the village 'The
Unicorn' looked down the slope to the cobbled
village square. Sightseers, delighting in the old
world charm, invaded the place in droves. This
year with the cold spring and wet weather the
village was quiet, left with its 'untouched for
centuries' look. There are certainly parts of 'The
Unicorn', the oldest pub in the area, which are not
of these times. The stone paved floor with grooves
worn by many feet, gave credence to an age where
needs had been simpler and quite foreign to folk
using it present day.

Genna watched as Issy, having swamped her with hugs and kisses over the bar, warmed her hands at the open log fire, sparkling and crackling in a vast inglenook fireplace. As the leggy Boxer bitch, obviously Fifi, shook rain from her coat, she looked disdainfully around and sneezed at the tang of wood smoke.

"Do I really look slimmer?"

"You look slimmer. Why would I say so otherwise?" Genna smiled.

"Oh, cheer me up, make me feel better about myself, I suppose. I actually looked like a hag not so long ago - skin and bone after Steve, but you know me, I eat for England mostly. I think I'm in better shape now."

Genna polished glasses, replaced bottles and put out fresh mats and ashtrays as Issy wriggled herself onto a bar stool, stuck out her chest and pulled in her stomach. A tight fitting top confirmed her idea of herself, Genna noticed.

Fifi stretched out her too big puppy paws in front of her before settling down to enjoy the warmth of the fire.

Genna regarded her friend carefully and reflected that Issy's face, framed by wings of red brown hair had certainly lost some of its chubbyness and appeared more oval and appealing. It suited her. Genna wondered if Issy saw changes in her from when they had last met over a year ago. As usual she did not have to wait long for Issy's view.

"You're looking terrific, Genna. I wish I could

hang onto a shape like Halle Berry. Mother's cooking will turn me into a sumo wrestler any day now."

"There's a lot of exercise in my life and that's the easy part. I don't really have time to stop and snack, or eat big meals. The manual work would make Olympic training seem a doddle."

"You're still helping out as much as ever?"

"You bet. It's a very healthy life." Genna rolled her eyes but was not really sorry for herself.

"I just seemed crazy you should leave school when you were so brilliant. Nobody could understand it."

"Dad left it up to me but I could see how up against it he was. What else could I do? Mother tried to persuade me to stay on. She does the accounts and knows all about shortage of money and labour. I felt I would let him down. Anyway more work would have settled on her shoulders. Dad just eats, sleeps and breathes farming and I would be the one to make things work that much better."

Issy's face took on a serious look. "I remember doing the big sister stuff when you had school problems. You listened to me as though I were Solomon."

"Oh, you were quite an idol. I wanted to be like you."

"Like me! You must have been mad. I'm a lunatic - still am!"

"But you didn't care - you'd just grab your

opportunities, go for things and get what you wanted."

"It's called selfishness! That's me alright."

"Genna's look was determined. Don't kid yourself I've given up on what I want, I'll get back to an education somehow when we're over the hump." But Genna knew the hump was getting bigger, would she ever have time for things she loved like music and serious reading? Mostly she ran out of hours and was too tired from the physical work which was always round the next farm corner.

Pete Murgatroyd, the landlord of 'The Unicorn', had been quick to see Genna's worth. His eyes had travelled over her figure, thick dark hair and clear blue eyes. He saw a winner to pull in customers. Later he watched her easy manner and the sensible way she coped with drunks and the awkward squad without antagonising them.

"So what about your brother? Does he like the idea of country doctoring after the big city."

"I think he loves it - like father. Dear Deborah doesn't. I think she's cooled a bit of late."

"The airhostess, she's really got her hooks into him?"

"I don't know about hooks, her sexual chemistry is as strong as car clamps. She's here next week-end. We have to sort the stream before she lands. She looks so terrific, but she's a real buzzard to everyone but Wills. I warned him she won't arrive in a Lear jet... on a broomstick more like. His face was a picture. I did promise to round up help for this week-end. Are you on?"

"What for?"

"Digging, diverting the stream away from the drive."

"Sure, why not, I'm pretty good at digging."

"William'll be pleased. He may drop in later."

"Fifi lifted a sleepy head as the pub door opened and banged in the wind, as a dark suited, professional looking person came through it.. He slid out of a navy overcoat as it dripped onto the stone floor. He turned with an apologetic smile. Genna was compelled to stare, the smile was Hollywood, magnetic. His eyes seemed to beam out a scarcely hidden warmth of approval as he took in the two striking girls. She smiled a welcome. "Rotten night. What can I get you?"

"Awful. He ran a hand through already tousled dark curly hair. "Larger, please," he pointed.

Genna was amused that Issy, elegantly perched on the bar stool, long legs crossed, had her mouth hanging open. Shutting it quickly, she struggled for composure and turned towards Genna as the young man made his way to the end of the bar.

"Who's that?" She mouthed silently.

"Could be the estate agents' new manager." Genna had her back to the company as she replied remembering Bessie's sex on a stick description.

The door banged again and Fifi looked up in disgust then staggered to her feet, bottom wagging furiously. The new comer bent to greet her, fair, wet hair flopped over his forehead above firm even features. His grey sweater was damp across the shoulders. Genna's stomach gave a lurch as she recognised Issy's brother. He looked older than she remembered. The laugh lines were more of a man's but his presence had lost none of the old magic.

"Wills, we've just been talking about you." Issy told him.

William looked down at his socks as though checking all was in order, then gave his attention to the company. "Bloody weather! Can I get you two a drink?" He looked from his sister towards Genna.

"G. and T. please. Genna do you remember my brother, Will? This is Angenna Mcfaiden from school. She used to come to tea. She was the clever one."

Genna shook the proffered hand, stretched up to find glasses and caught William's eye following her movement as her black sweater tightened over the full rounded shape above her slim waist, a silver locket as her only adornment. His gaze lingered as though he were reluctant to turn away. Such attention was not something that usually bothered Genna but now she found herself colouring.

"WELL!, Dr. Farrington!"

William turned as the dark haired charmer from the other end of the bar came towards him. He frowned before recognition dawned. "God Almighty! John! It must be ten years since I set eyes on you. I can hardly believe it. How're you doing?" The pair shook hands warmly.

"Really good. In the village with Summers and

Goldthorpe."

"You're not going to tell me that slinky looking Merc's yours, the one that parks and grid locks the village of late?"

"Fraid so." John looked sheepish. Property's booming around here, to the detriment of the locals, I'm afraid."

"You could be the very man I need to see." William went on to describe his house buying intentions and Issy rolled nightmare eyes at Genna.

The four legged member of the party now quite aroused from her slumbers, slid over to John, her behind gyrating like a belly dancer. John bent down to stroke the dog. Fifi, white spats and bib dazzling against her bright brindle coat, flirted outrageously.

"You're a smart young lady." John scratched Fifi's back like a man who appreciated dogs, Genna noticed, thereby guaranteeing himself a place in Issy's esteem like nothing else could.

"Fifi! Behave yourself. You're a complete tart!"

Fifi ignoring the command, rolled on her back, paws waving in the air to the amusement of the group.

"I don't believe you've met my sister, Isobelle. William commented dryly, "or her friend Angenna Mcfaiden. A much nicer girl. Even though she used to have a habit of throwing her cake on the floor when she came to tea."

Genna, momentarily unnerved, caught the humour sparkling in William's eyes and bent over the bar, doubling up with mirth. "I made sure you'd forgotten," she gasped wiping her eyes and pushing dark strands of hair behind her ears.

"Never, you practically batted it into mother's lap. I had all on not to shout with laughter. Issy had never brought such an entertaining friend home. "

Genna felt her insides turn to jelly all over again at the smile playing over his handsome features. She turned away to hid the emotion carrying her along its wave crest.

"This, by the way, is John Glendenning, a ne're do well I went to school with." William gestured to John. "Come to think of it, not only could you advise on the housing market, you could be useful on Sunday; how's your digging?"

John looked suitably baffled. Issy was quick to explain. "He's dragging people in from the street to help us stop the stream flooding our drive. Only Genna's volunteered so far. You could be the next to get lucky, John."

"Sounds like a party...count me in. John grinned good naturedly. "You must excuse me now I have to dash. Call in and give me time and place, William," he turned to the girls with a sexy grin "and I'm all yours... er don't listen to any wild tales William tells you about me, he's sure to exaggerate." So saying he grabbed his coat and headed for the door.

Genna stole a look at Issy, who appeared to be breathing electrically charged air which had now reverted to normal everyday stuff. "Gees, Wills," she exclaimed before the door had hardly shut, "what are you going to exaggerate for us?"

"Exaggerate? Don't need to...he was always tripping over girls, he had every female within a five mile radius of school hot for his body, while all we caught were sticklebacks... an early developer, you might say.. Where's the gents removed to?"

"It's over there," Genna pointed. "The door's been altered." The two girls exchanged amused glances as William headed in that direction. "Your brother is really something." Genna commented.

He doesn't miss much the only person he has been fooled by is that Debora. But what about John Glendenning?"

"Let's hope **he's** not a knicker chaser, like in licking more than one lolly at a time." Genna 's, serious face crinkling with fun, turning her into a picture of attractiveness.

Issy joined in then sighed. "I just could not cope with another of those after Steve. He would have shagged anything on two feet. What about you, Genna, no steady boyfriend?"

"Not much choice or time. There was Bobby Smailes used to help dad in the busy times and we'd sneak off down to the woods, you know, Badgers Dyke, to look for cubs in the dark? It was really fun at first."

"And did you see any?"

"No, we were too busy snogging. Then he got too rough. I slapped him hard and dashed for home. I think he sent word around I was a non-starter, a tease or something." Genna shrugged, seemingly unconcerned about her sullied reputation amongst the youth of the village. She hesitated, realising she did not have to hide the truth from Issy."Actually, Issy, it wasn't quite like that; he changed from being the friendly sort to something horribly different. He was a burley guy even then, pinned me down so that I couldn't move. His nails raked the top of my thighs and he tore my pants off trying to get inside... Issy, it was the worst moment of my life... heading for rape. I was terrified."

"Genna looked down at the bar shuddering at the memory. "Before worse happened my knee must have caught him...in the googlies. I struggled desperately to get out from underneath him... There was blood all over my legs when I arrived home and I had to burn my pants. If mum had got wind of it she would have gone hairless. Anyway it was a real turn off sex. Fancy being nineteen and still a virgin."

Genna, you poor thing, what a ghastly experience." Issy's concern was genuine.

"Y'know, I think I'm through it now; I can talk about it without wanting to run and hide." Genna smiled changing the subject quickly. "When did you say we were digging the stream? That could be interesting."

"Sunday. Yes... it could."

CHAPTER THREE

By the time Genna drove up to 'The Rectory' on Sunday morning the team diverting the stream appeared to have departed to set about their task. The silver blue Mercedes sports owned by John Glendenning was parked at the front of the house but there was no sign of the diggers. Genna looked beyond 'The Rectory' towards the silent woods on 'The Croft' land. There was nothing to be heard except a lone bird glorying in the morning.

She climbed the few steps to the front door flanked by its laurel bushes. Behind the Victoria glass panes she could see movement. She was about to ring the bell when the door was opened by Issy's mother.

"Genna, how lovely to see you. You missed the coffee. Like a cup before you join the chain gang?" Marjorie Farrington raised an eyebrow as though she was only just tolerating all this nonsense.

Genna knew differently, the attractive older woman had been more that capable of coping with anything her family had thrown at her. As the wife of the local doctor she had a reputation for having an understanding ear.

"Thanks but no, I've missed the action already. Where do I look to find them?"

"Back down the drive on the right through the trees...Oh and Genna we're very grateful for your help. The stream has been a darn nuisance lately. What with global warming and more flooding likely, I'm pleased William has decided to take matters into his own hands, even though Harvey's sceptical."

Genna turned her back on the house, walking the way she had come. Looking now towards the wood she saw what she had missed when driving, the stream had left a long swathe of debris where it had flooded and encroached onto the drive.

The grass was long and wet as she struck out following the course of the water twisting between the trees and she was glad of her Wellingtons as she went deeper into the wood.

Daffodils were beginning to unfold yellow heads beneath branches with fresh green buds, some already bursting out with crumpled tiny leaves. The feel and sight of Spring and could not be ignored. A smell of freshly dug earth drifted her way and ahead she heard voices.

"Fifi, you stupid dog, I'm covering me from head to foot." Issy looked up as Genna approached. "Gen, thank heavens you've arrived. Look at this juvenile animal, she thinks she's going to find Australia."

"Hi, Issy. Where are the rest of the workers?" Genna smiled as the bespattered Issy wiped soil from her face and hair.

"Over there in the trees. They're digging a new course away from the drive. I'm suppose to move the earth ready to fill in the old stream bed when we divert."

"They've obviously worked out the

technicalities."

"Oh, sure, for ages before we started they were plotting the course like a cavalry charge. Come and say hello. Maybe they'll be ready to stop for a breather."

Following her, Genna took in Issy's fashionable combat trousers and chunky beige sweater. She looked down at her own worn jeans and faded blue anorak suddenly wishing her clothes did not look so old. Something touched her hand and she looked down to see Fifi, her white paws filthy with soil, wagging her stumpy tail in welcome. Somehow it reassured her. Dogs knew who was worth having.

"HANGFIRE, GUYS, REINFORCEMENTS HAVE ARRIVED". Issy yelled through the trees to where the two in the ditch looked up from their digging.

"Genna, what a marvellous excuse for a rest. Thanks for coming." William stood up as they drew near.

Genna noted with some satisfaction that both John and William were wearing old jeans and dark T shirts, (their sweaters having been discarded as they dug) making her feel more at home She did her best to look unconcerned but in truth, under Williams discerning gaze her whole being seemed to quiver. He was looking at her, damp blond hair falling over his face. The very essence of his lean body made her feel weak.

"You look very clean, but we'll soon fix that." He lent on his spade, while John, who having said hello, was talking seriously to Issy. William continued. "We hope to take this straight down the hill and join up with the stream nearer the bottom, thereby taking out the bend that floods the drive." He pointed back to the newly dug earth.

"Sounds like sense to me, but William, isn't this 'Croft' land?" Genna asked.

"That has been the sticking point, but 'The Croft' is a boarded up shell. Father tried to talk to old Mrs. Gatenby when she was alive, he even wrote. She replied through solicitors to say she would not allow any boundaries or land to be disturbed and she would take action for trespass if they were."

William sat down on a large rock in front of them and patted the place beside him. Genna noticed the strong sinews of his neck where blond hair changed into smooth brown skin disappearing into his T shirt. Her insides did some more quivering as she joined him.

"What a weird old soul. Do you think she was deranged?" She asked, reminding herself to be cool and realistic.

"Sometimes old people survive in the most appalling conditions, even with money to provide otherwise, when senility, or depression take over but... amazingly enough, this was not the case so father said."

"He found her of course, yes, I remember now."

"Well the house looked decrepit from the outside but apparently the inside was immaculate, clean and fresh. He decided she had all her chairs at home."

Diary Notes: WINTER. 1937.

Father is ill again. January and February were always bad months for him. I have been summoned home from school. Mother said of late he has spent a lot of time in his retreat, his own special hideout. He lies there on the day bed and has everything to hand so that he does not get out of breath. There must be many like him who suffer from the effects of mustard gas.

I have been to visit him in hospital. He is in an oxygen tent and looks dreadful. Mother says it reminds her of Africa and when they had to sleep in mosquito nets. When I came near he felt for my hand and as I drew close he whispered to me that mother would find it difficult on her own and I must look after her. He obviously thinks he is going to die. Poor, dear father.

It has happened as anticipated, father has died. I cried all day but it made my eyes very red and puffy, so I tried hard to stop. Mother seemed to pull down some sort of shutter over the one she already has in place, so I was astonished when she put her arm around me and said she needed me at home. I shall be taken out of boarding school and learn some house husbandry, she says.

I don't know whether I am delighted at the freedom or despondent in some ways to have to live solely with mother. I shall look forward to the summer and a visit from Rory and Tom. They have both written excited letters mostly about flying. Rory put 'with fondest love' at the end of his. I wanted to cry again but instead kissed his name.

Genna had helped Issy for the best part of ten minutes in her job of moving soil to eventually damn the stream. The ground was soft and heavy with water, even so it was   easy to dig into.

That same morning Genna has been up early to get ahead with her jobs. Her mother had encouraged her to go when she had been reluctant to leave, reminding her she seldom had time to herself.

William and John appeared to be involved in decision making. "What the hell are they chewing over up there?" Issy wanted to know.

Genna was well aware that Issy, impatient as usual, was looking forward to talking to John. For all her remarks about the kind of men who were bad news, she was attracted to John's dark good looks and easy manner like iron filings to a magnet.

"I saw William point to that big rock we were sitting on. I bet they're deciding which way to reroute the stream to avoid it."

"Of course, why don't I have your brand of common sense?" Issy sighed.

"Come on, let's go and see if that is the hold up."

"It goes down a lot deeper than we imagined. I thought we maybe able to upend it but there isn't a hope, it juts out underneath." Willim pointed to the offending rock at his feet.

"The obvious way round it by that big clump of daffodils." John nodded in their direction.

"It's quite a massive clump but if we disturb them we can take plenty of earth and replant them. William stuck his spade into the ground. "What about this line?"

John nodded in agreement. "Will you clear the earth as we dig girls, then we won't need to stand on the daffodils. Fifi move over." He shoved the dog's backside out of the way, his figure almost stocky beside William's height. The dog was snuffling into a hole she was attending to and making a noise as though she was suffocating in the process.

"I think she's scented a rabbit." Issy offered, as grass and small sods flew while Fifi dug, bottom up, paws moving like a paddle steamer.

"Issy, what the hell has she found?" Look, she's got it in her mouth. Take it off her."

Issy did her best to entice the dog towards her but the young bitch was ready for a game and danced away. Genna, seeing her chance when Fifi came backing towards her, grabbed a firm hold on her neck. "Give it up, Fifi! Drop." The animal did exactly as she was told and looked up at Genna eagerly. The object was wet from the dogs mouth and the soggy earth. "I think it's an old key case. It's on the point of disintegrating."

"Now we're getting some sense. Let's have a good look." William came over to where Genna was standing, holding the object in her hand, away from an eager Fifi.

"It's coming apart - there's a key inside. It's amazing it's not more rusted judging from the state of the case. I suppose the leather's protected it to some extent. It's quite a big key and the shape's impressive." William turned the key over slowly in his hand then gave it back in its tatty case to Genna. "Hang on to it, Genna, until we've finished here and we'll take another look."

Genns stuffed the sodden object into her anorak pocket and picked up her spade once more. The group, assisted by the dog, recommenced digging deep to the side of the boulder to cope with the flow of water they expected.

It was Issy who found the first bone and tossed it carelessly to one side. The dog dived after it. The air was heavy with the smell of damp earth and leaf mould.

"What now?" William looked up, reluctant to be put off again from digging.

"It's only an old bone... and there's another... just a minute....OH, MY GOD!

Genna felt a cold sensation at the back of her neck at the implications of what was happening. She watched as Issy bent down on her hands and knees, intent on clearing more earth and small sods, but finding more than she bargained for. The pitch of her voice made William move quickly. **"Look... here... Will."** He was soon by her side peering down.

"Oh, Jesus! ... No," he murmured quietly as the

others stood looking to where they had been digging.

Issy brushed earth from her fingers in horrified disbelief as to where they had been. "Well, I don't know about Jesus, but it's a somebody, that's for sure,"

The remains they had uncovered, as far as Genna could see as she took another hurried look, must have been buried only a few feet deep. A skull lay partially revealed about to leer at them. Issy had at first disturbed a hand resting on top of what had been a body."

"Well, he's long since past caring about who he was, or how he got there. I'd better go and telephone the police." William told the silent shocked company.

It occurred to Genna that William, as a doctor, could take death and remains in his stride, and was more concerned about the hold up in the digging, while Issy, also used to such things, was quiet and pale as though she's seen a ghost but then she had dug her fingers into a muddy eye socket.

It was a solemn group carrying their spades, making there way back to 'The Rectory'. Once inside William took charge. "Let's get our priorities right. I think we need a drink," he told them, leading the way to the sitting room. "Mother will be in the kitchen. I won't tell her yet or she may start doing back somersaults." He winked at Genna as he took her anorak.

The room was exactly as Genna remembered,

along with the chocolate cake, unpretentiously elegant and comfortable with a fire burning contentedly in the grate. A midnight blue velvet suite sat on the deep swirls of an Indian carpet. Tall bookshelves filled an alcove next to the fireplace and there was a high rounded bay with an inviting window seat where one could look out down the drive and to the woods beyond.

"This is going to be a right jamboree! We shall be invaded by the law, archaeologists - God knows what else." Issy ran her hand through her hair, rolling her eyes at John.

"Looks like William's attempt to divert the stream'll by stymied. Everything will be cordoned off while they dig out the rest of him." John nodded in agreement.

"Have you any idea who it could be, Issy? I suppose it matters how long it's been there as to whether there's a murder enquiry." Genna concluded.

"Murder! Of course. No wonder she never wanted people messing about on her land... but I've no idea who. So far as I know there's never been a man up there. I've been thinking stone age burials, there's so much history in these parts. That **will** mean endless questions. William will love having a murder enquiry on his hands if they're still here next weekend and Debora arrives."

"I hope it won't matter we've been digging on somebody else's land. After all it was to prevent a hazard." Genna replied, trying to lose sight of the

Debora bit.

Issy went on to explain to John the problems they'd had with Emily Gatenby and at that point William returned with hot toddies for everyone.

"The local Constabulary have to get in touch with Kettlington. They want to ask questions. I wouldn't be surprised if they send the CID and the drug squad," he handed out steaming drinks to Genna and John. "I'm sure you two will be OK. But I wouldn't like to vouch for Issy." He raised a mocking eybrow at the gravity of it.

Issy took the next drink from him and frowned. "I hope for your sake they've sorted it before next weekend which is unlikely and you'll have Debora AND the press to contend with," she replied waspishly by way of retaliation.

CHAPTER FOUR

It was as Issy had anticipated, the police had arrived in droves, blocking 'The Rectory' drive, cordoning off areas here and covering up things there.

It became obvious that they did not regard 'The Elvingdale Four' as murders, but nevertheless asked a good many questions. William was grilled about why he was digging on 'Croft' land and had given them the details of the wayward stream and how it was a hazard to his father and himself when going to visit patients.

"Oh yes, they got that one in and the police seemed to be happy with the answer." Issy told Genna on the 'phone.

William had made it plain at the outset that John and Genna were not really involved but could be contacted when and if necessary. The police had not detained them long but were more interested in what William and Issy could tell them.

"Did we know Miss Gatenby well? Did she have many men friends? Did you ever see any of her visitors? Well, of course she hated the whole damn human race. Even Geoff Cordingly with the milk only ever saw her once a blue flood."

"I can see there won't be an end to this for a quite a while." Genna murmured.

"Quite. I just hope we get to hear the details when they've done more work on the body. So far all they've come up with is that it's a man by the shape of the pelvis and, he was buried in some sort of thick coat. I'll keep you up to pace with anything and, Genna, keep your eyes and ears open at the pub. Locals are sure to know something they wouldn't dream of telling the police. You know how buttoned up they can be here."

Genna did indeed keep her eyes and ears open. The village fair hummed with activity and gossip in the aftermath of the discovery. Much clucking and muttering went on, particularly after Yorkshire Television's Outside Broadcast Unit arrived in force with snaking black cables and men shouldering cameras like sacks of coal. They shot odd angles of the village and sneaked up the drive to 'The Rectory' where the law stopped them.

Police infiltrated all corners of the area. As Genna steered the truck through the stone walled lanes to the village no less than three wasp-like cars either drew out of side roads or presented themselves as an obstacle to pass.

There was an air of expectancy in the pub where crumbs of information were exchanged and magnified to dubious good purpose by the lunch time drinkers.

"Lookin' for more bodies, tha knows. Where there's one tha's sure to be two, like sheep and kids crossing the road."

"Aye', it'll be affectin' water supply afore too long, disturbin things an' all dysentery, typhoid, all them diseases. Tea tasted funny this morning."

At least they could be right about digging for

more bodies, Genna acknowledged to herself, ignoring the rest.

The newspaper brigade had also arrived, complete with photographic big guns. They found their way to the pub fairly quickly, awaiting information or something else to materialise. Genna was there first target for questions.

"Lived here long have you, love?" The first one lit his cigarette, noting her wholesome attractiveness through lizard's eyes, as they sought crumbs of information to turn into headlines.

"Not here, I live further up the Dale."

"Did you know ol' girl up at 'The Croft' then, or any of her friends?"

Genna shook her head and was silent. When they had gone it occurred to her she did know somebody who knew Emily Gatenby and that somebody was old Mrs. Clarke. She had worked for the family for years and lived only strides away from the pub. Maybe she could have earned herself some money she reflected, had she been willing to hint at such a name. But she knew she would not want to be responsible for subjecting the old lady to a barrage of questions. However, there was nothing to stop her visiting Mrs. Clarke herself and finding out if she wanted to talk about old times.

The rest of the day had been a slog of farm errands in between her other job of driving a minibus to take the village children to school in

Kettlington and collecting them later. There had been no time to visit Mrs. Clarke that day. When she had arrived back at the farm her mother greeted her at the yard door.

"Genna, the washers packed up this morning. I was too busy and I had to leave it. Your father had a go but it's no good - it's still full of water and dirty washing. He said to wait until the man came but that could be heaven knows when."

Genna took in her mother's tired drawn face. She could see something of her own likeness in the slight, curly haired figure. Her resolve had hardened. She could cope.

"Don't worry, Mum, I'll get it out easily enough and do it be hand. It won't take long." She saw her mother's shoulders relax. "Put the kettle on and we'll have a cuppa before we start. I'll go and get changed."

Genna knew it would be ages before anyone came to see the washer. The farm was quite isolated - well off the road, making it an expedition for any repair man, but more to the point, was the cost of a call out for them.

Walking along the passage to her bedroom, the wooden floor sloped drunkenly to one side where the old farmhouse had subsided over the years into the contours of the land. The bedroom itself was large but chill with the feel of damp and poverty. The carpet had lost most of its pattern and colour. A rag rug covered a threadbare patch worn through in parts to the floorboards. Genna had been meaning to take the lot up and varnish the floor but so far she had not found time. A long bookcase lurched against one wall with shelves that had been added as the number of books grew.

She began to change, shivering in the draughts that whistled their way around the skirting boards. A single bar electric fire to warm the room on winter mornings reminded her of a candle in a cowshed.

Her reflection in the mirror sitting on top of a big old fashioned chest of drawers told her she looked tired and she was aware of the sense of frustration that had dogged her more than ever of late.

Where was it all leading to? How long could she go on doing this? If she left her parents she had no training to make enough money to support herself and help them. She may find a husband but at the moment that was as far away as China. Of the men she knew, Pete Murgatroyd, the landlord of 'The Unicorn', came to mind. He had a roving eye and it often came to rest on Genna. He was obviously discreet about outside conquests, in fact he seemed well attached to his marriage. Perhaps his sexual appetite was larger than what was offered at home. Genna had the feeling she could be on the menu for snacks should she be so inclined. That would be disaster. It would distress her father badly if he found her to be a marriage breaker and only add more trouble to her mother's overburdened life.

Her thoughts turned to William, a habit she seemed to have acquired of late. Could that be the source of her pent up feelings? His understated humour and air of absent minded casualness seemed to get under her skin and she wanted so much more of him, ached to get to know him properly, something she would probably never do. She recalled how serious he looked sometimes but with the perceptive smiling eyes that held understanding.

"Tea's ready, Gen." She could hear her mother's voice floating up from the kitchen as she peeled off her sweater quickly, still thinking of William. The curves of her nineteen year old body, even fully clothed produced reactions in most men. William was used to naked patients but what sort of person would he see her as, a country hick, bar help, farm labourer, driving kids to school? What difference did it make that she hoped for more education. Nine GCSEs had come easily with high grades and only time to work in spasms.

There was the other side of the coin, the side her mother saw. The suicide rate amongst Dales' farmers and even in other parts of the country, was high. Farming was suffering badly, causing a major cause for concern in the country areas. Genna sensed dread in her mother and that she was torn between husband's and daughter's future.

It all added to the fact she had to put her life on hold and resist taking the opportunities the world offered. The hopeless knot of frustration tightened itself in her gut as she struggled into working clothes. Unusual tears of rage and self pity welled in her eyes as she thought of her restricted existence. She fastened her jeans and clenched her teeth against angry sobs at the cleft stick in which she was caught. She took a deep breath, held it and with determination, dragged a hand across wet lashes as she made her way to the door and her mother's call.

Diary notes.
1938.

It is not as nice at home as I really imagined. Mother and I ride out most mornings when the weather's good enough and sometimes we hunt. I really enjoy that. We take out the car to go to Kettlington to shop. Mother will never stop in Elvingdale in case people offer her sympathy over father's death. She says she could not bear it. I believe there is another aspect to it.

Since I left school I have lost contact with friends in the village. Mother did not approve of 'those' type of people and I know she has an element of determination that I should not become involved again with such company. Sometimes I long for friends and of course I talk to Marion. At other times I am really pleased I can just read where and what I want. One good thing is, mother says she is going to let me drive to Kettlington next week. Father has already taught me how to double de clutch but I have not had a lot of practice.

I write to Rory and Tom when they write to me. I spend ages trying to think of the interesting things to say; my life does not have anything very exciting in it as theirs does.

Their letters have mentioned the likelihood of war with Germany and Rory said Mr Chamberlain will be a peace maker and avert trouble. At the same time, he sounds as though he would rather enjoy it and says he wants to join the Royal Air Force soon, when he's eighteen. I cannot think about that. Perhaps it will never happen. I do not imagine war will affect us much here, way out in the Dales. It will all take place in Europe somewhere.

I do wonder if I will ever marry Rory. I know he is a cousin but I don't think that would matter. I hope that is what mother has planned for me. I am looking so forward to summer when they are due to stay. Sometimes I walk down to the place by the stream in the woods where Rory kissed me. I sit on the rock listening to the bird song and the water chortling over the stones, as I remember the touch of Rory's brown skin against my cheek and how blissful it felt when he kissed me.

It was some little time after finding the remains that Genna had the nightmare. She found herself alone walking through trees not far from where they had been digging. The night was dark with swirling mist. The shape of a tall figure caught her eye, moving from tree to tree in front of her. The figure she could see was dressed in a heavy coat with the collar turned up. She peered through the darkness trying to identify the person, yet at the same time, apprehensive about what she may find.

Without warning the figure suddenly slowed down so that she caught up with it. The shoulders turned menacingly and she shrieked with fear as she saw a white glowing skeletal head facing her, the bones contrasting sharply against the fabric of the dark coat.

"GO AWAY!" She heard herself scream as she awoke groping and thrashing at the bed clothes. With shaking hands she stretched out to turn on a bedside light. A stupid dream! She heaved a large breath and lay back once more on the pillow but that was not the end of it.

A few nights later she found herself in the same place. The ghastly figure was waiting for her. She reminded herself it was just a stupid dream. Just take no notice and look at him. This time as the figure turned towards her she stood still waiting, terrified as panic overtook her but curiosity was the winner. The skull grinned at her as he came nearer. She watched the coated arm rise slowly, a hand with two bones of its fingers missing where Issy must have disturbed them, held out something towards her.

Her feet were rooted, her legs WOULD NOT MOVE. She could not run away now if she tried. Again she heard herself shrieking "GO AWAY! NO... NO!" The spectre was determined and the bones of cold fingers came nearer to her face almost touching her cheek. She knew she would die if it touched her but she was cemented to the ground it was no use.

She awoke whimpering, limbs jerking. Breathing slowly to help things back to normal, she wondered if she had awakened her parents with the noisy shouting but she knew their bedroom was some way away and the walls thick. She tried to recall the details of the dream now she had stopped being scared. Something had been held out to her; the bony fingers had tried to make her take something. What on earth had it been. She had seen the thing, even recognised it, dangling inches from her face.

Of course, the memory returned in a rush. It was a key - THE KEY, the one she had stuffed in her anorak pocket and forgotten clean about after Fifi had dug it up just before the big find. Where was the jacket? She remembered dumping it on a hook behind the kitchen door and had not worn it since. She jumped out of bed, forgetting the cold and headed down the passage to the stairs, almost in her hurry, skidding into the wall where the floor tilted down.

The kitchen was warmer and her search was rewarded as she found the garment and felt the hardness of the metal object in the pocket The shock of finding the remains had resulted in them all forgetting what Fifi had found; obviously her subconscious had been working overtime to remind her.

Back in bed once more, she gazed at the key and the metal forming an outline of it's carefully shaped head, the shape of a Tudor rose in fact. Maybe it would tell them something about the family at 'The Croft' or more importantly shed light on the identity of the poor man in his thick coat buried in the ground.

CHAPTER FIVE

It was the following Monday evening when Genna, behind the bar of 'The Unicorn', began to set out her stall for any unlikely rush of early customers. She pushed newly washed, shiny hair off her face as she bent forward to wipe the counter.

She had hurried to get cleaned up after helping her father with a ewe struggling to give birth to difficult twins. It had been hard physical work with her hand sometimes buried inside the sheep. Even though Spring was well and truly here, lambs on hill farms were often timed to come later than those in lower pastures so they had a chance of surviving better after the cold, often wet conditions of the early season. The struggle had been worth it with two bloodied, slimy bodies breathing fresh air and beginning to stagger into life.

She cleaned the counter thinking of the look on her father's face; he had been a happy man and the bond between them as they had completed the job had been almost tangible. She looked up from wiping to see Issy appear through the door. "High, Issy, at last you've come out of hiding. " Has the dust settled at your end?" The police have been jumping out of the floorboards hereabouts."

"God, Genna, we could be through the worst but none of it's to be recommended. Talk about an intrusion of privacy, they do everything but look up your nose and in your ears." Issy slid out of her coat and onto the bar stool.

Genna laughed at Issy's outrage. "Same here, searchers for the truth all over the place complete with cameras and notebooks."

"I have so much to tell you, I'm nearly exploding."

"Great. A drink? Vodka and blackcurrant?"

"Why not? Have one with me?"

"Thanks, fruit juice - have to keep a clear head."

"The thing is, the forensic team have told William the body could have been there for something over fifty years, back to possibly the 1940s." Issy waved a hand triumphantly.

"You mean we're celebrating because, not being around then it lets us off the hook as murder suspects?"

"You bet. There were remains of flesh on the bones underneath the coat. Apparently due to the chemical composition of the ground: corpses rot at different rates...but more significantly for them, there is no obvious signs of an injury that could have caused death."

Genna pulled a grim face "Not clouted over the head or stabbed through the heart?"

"Sort of thing. Even so all this still puts us not one jot nearer finding out who the guy was, or how he got there."

Genna was about to confine to Issy her nightmare story of her recovery of the key from her anorak pocket, when Issy under a full head of steam, set off on another tack.

"The other business is about William and

Debora."

Genna felt her inside tighten up with apprehension as to what Issy may be about to tell her and all thoughts of the key were left behind.

"She landed Saturday, like a Dahlia in a cabbage patch, short black skirt, neat little jacket, pale blonde hair against her perfect complexion and, with charming disdain, made us all feel like a bunch of frumps. I forgot to mention the long legs, staggering heels and perfect figure."

"It must be pretty quaggy at your place what with the stream and the police cars." Genna tried to sidestep the gorgeous image. "How did William cope?"

"To be fair, the police mostly parked at 'The Croft' and came down through the wood but the stream was still like a river and William did go out with Wellingtons and Mack for Debora in case they had trouble getting up the drive. But that's not what I'm going to tell you. The rain caused havoc in another direction."

Genna waited wondering what was coming.

"Mother put Debora in my room because the guest room had a drip. She had stuck a pan underneath it and knew I wouldn't mind sleeping there. Honestly, the sacrifices I make for family. Anyway I came in late, or rather early morning after a booze up with the girls in Kettlington and went up to bed. Fifi must have heard me. She often sneaks upstairs and we have a scuffle. I hide under the duvet and she has to find me. So into my room she goes and jumps on the bed. If that had been all it may have been alright...but."

Genna could feel her heart thumping in dread of what was coming next and wished Issy would stop telling her.

"Of course William had visited and was in bed with her just about to get passionate. Fi jumps ecstatically into the middle of them and tries to lick Debora's ears off. She, I might tell you, practically had hysterics looking up into Fi's slavering chops. Talk about three in this marriage. William tried to calm her, I tried to calm Fifi. Debora commented sarcastically that he should have sold tickets!"

Oh, Issy! What a pickle! Genna chuckled in spite of her dismay at the situation.

"She did not come down to breakfast next morning and I couldn't keep my face straight when I tried to apologise to William for Fifi's behaviour. They departed very po faced with each other. With a bit of luck..." Issy rubbed her hands together, her too big mouth breaking into a wide grin, "could be it won't last."

Genna prayed she was right but did not dare to hope and instead changed the conversation. "What about John? I bet you're dying to drag him off to your lair, rip his shirt off and anything else that gets in the way of taking full possession."

"You reckon that would be cool? Is that how you think I should play it?"

"Me? What do I know about anything? You're the one who dishes it out and get what she wants."

"And the knocks. Actually William's playing squash with John after surgery and they're coming here pretty soon...so I may be able to work on him." Issy swept a hand through her hair.

The now familiar frisson fizzled through Genna at the thought of seeing William, what's more if Issy cornered John, maybe William would talk to her. She prayed some more, this time that the pub would not be busy.

Diary Notes
1938

I have had a letter from Rory saying that he has applied to join the Royal Air Force and they are not able to visit this Summer. I was so miserable after reading it, mother even asked what was wrong with me but I managed to about face and brush my feelings aside for her benefit.

Rory thinks he will be accepted easily because he has already learned to fly. Tom is about to do the same thing the minute he is eighteen. Rory has promised to write more and tell me all that happens, so I do not feel completely let down. It is just that I will not be able to watch the Spring unfold in the woods with such joy knowing that soon I would be sharing it with Rory.

My driving is much better now mother has allowed me to practise. The first time I forgot to steer properly while changing gear. I nearly ran over a woman on a Belisha crossing in Kettlington, that was BEFORE bouncing over the kerb. Mother told me to get a grip on myself or she would not allow me to drive again. In the lanes around here It doesn't matter if I hit the verges but I must be more careful where there are people not to knock them over.

Marion and I had such a giggle about my driving. I shall miss her terribly when she leaves. She is not a lot older than me but she's getting married. I expect mother will have to find someone else to help in the house.

I am sure Rory really cares about me. He wrote how he would miss seeing my lovely eyes and the air of calm I radiate. I sat on the rock in raptures thinking about this. It protected me for ages from that one horrid word, namely WAR!

By the time William and John arrived after squash. Genna realised there was no hope she would get to talk to William on his own. The local population had turned out in bigger numbers than usual for a Monday, probably to discuss their particular contribution to the new found fame of the village, as far as Genna could see.

The Farringtons and John had tucked themselves into a corner next to the bar.

"Have to learn to keep my head down so as not to be accosted by grateful, or not so grateful patients." William commented to Genna when she had a minute between serving customers. At the same moment a ruggedly handsome bearded man appeared through the door at the back of the bar. The head was followed by the broad shoulders and powerful body of Pete Murgatroyd, the landlord of 'The Unicorn'.

"You OK there, Gen? I'm supposed to be off to the Fell Rescue meeting, but it's bloody busy for a Monday."

"You go, Pete - it'll soon quieten down. I've served most of this lot."

"Don't be taking any lip from that rough bunch," he nodded in the direction of the group in the corner near the bar, then faking surprise, "beggin you pardon, folks, didn't recognise the good doctor and his friend. You could be well looked after, Gen, if we have any rowdies in." He tipped an imaginary cap in the direction of the three, only letting his face slip into its normal good humour as he touched Genna lightly on the shoulder. "Cheers, love, you're a star...see you in my dreams." He winked at Genna.

"Believe he's quite a character, that one, so I've heard, ready to risk life and limb for the foolhardy?" William watched as Pete departed and Genna pulled a pint.

"Nothing mad, bad or stupid," she shrugged, "he's clued up when it comes to fell rescue ... saves lives." She hesitated choosing her words carefully. "In lots of ways he's ... a really good guy." It was not exactly what she wanted to say but decided discretion was best when it came to Pete's wandering eye.

William raised an eyebrow and she wondered if he already knew that Pete was not always such a good guy. There was a lull in trade. Should she tell him about the nightmare and the key?" She really should have told somebody. Too late she realised John had taken his attention and Issy was busting with some new snippet.

"Genna!" (Issy managed to keep it down to an excited stage whisper.) "We're going walking on Sunday on the fells, **a whole day out.** Isn't he wickedly gorgeous? **I simply cannot wait."**

"Hope he gets back alive." Genna commented. "Issy, I can see you're airborne at the prospect of this invitation and I'm delighted but could you just touch the floor for a minute, I have a confession to make."

"Of course, I'm on about me again, fire away."

The nightmare and its consequences were duly related. With wide eyes Issy gave the tale her full attention. "Shit, Genna, do you realise we've been withholding evidence from the police." Issy giggled happily. Do you think we ought to keep it all zipped, or tell William... what do you think?

"Issy, *for heavens sake* don't tell him. I'll feel an idiot and it cannot be that important, it wasn't on the body. Let's just keep it to ourselves."

"What do I think about what?" William was all there.

"Do you think they've any more ideas about who bony Joe was?" Issy came back nonchalantly.

"Issy don't be so brash about dead people and

no, I don't think they have." William frowned fully aware that he was being sidetracked and not liking it. He turned back to his conversation with John.

"Listen," Genna bent forward conspiratorially, "there's old Mrs. Clarke, she lives just a hop away from the pub. I'll pay her a visit sometime soon and see whether she knows anything."

"That's brilliant, Gen, I shall give you a bell later in the week and see how you've got on."

Undressing in the cold bedroom, Genna thought of her cynical 'hope he gets out alive' comment to Issy. She was not, she told herself, usually cynical but maybe it was a touch of sour grapes, after all weren't the ideas of ravaging John simply her own fantasies about William? If she were truthful. The difference was, Issy would think it and go for it and she would only think.

A small ginnel led between cottages just off the cobbles village square; it twisted along an ivy covered wall with the end of a cottage providing the other side in making the narrow passage. As Genna found her way along the path, she remembered it opened onto a square. Blocked off by a stand of trees on the right and a high stone wall on the left, in the middle a row of cottages stood facing her. The whole formed a sheltered backwater, the late afternoon sun shining through the trees.

The cottages themselves had low walled gardens at their front with Gilly flowers newly bursting into velvet array, others had window boxes with bright spring blooms nodding and tumbling out of them. A wave of grassy floral perfume drifted towards Genna as she approached.

She was looking for something she had always admired and spotted quickly because it stood out from the rest, namely a fox's head knocker gleaming in the yellow light. She picked it up and tapped it against the door then waited.

Turning back to the scene she reflected at what a small Shangri-la she was looking at. The roofs were softened with lichen, their outline blurred against majestic trees, green cathedrals where birds trilled high songs from their own choir stalls.

A shuffling noise made Genna turn back to the door sharply. She heard what she imagined to be locks and chains being undone, perhaps by stiff old fingers. A crack appeared as the door opened a fraction and a pair of watery but bright eyes looked at her, alerts and wary of intruders. The fact that old people were mugged in their homes had not escaped this one's notice. She was being sized up through the gap.

"N' then, luv, I'm slow, this chains the very devil to unhook with them fingers of mine. What does thee want?"

"Hello, Mrs. Clarke, it's Genna. Remember me, I used to bring you eggs from the farm when I was smaller?"

"Good God! Young Genna McFaiden. Tha's grown

into such a fine lass I didn't recognise thee." The door opened with miraculous speed and a quite tall and thin old lady stood before her, beckoning her inside, Mrs. Marion Clarke, no less.

CHAPTR SIX.

Mrs. Clarke may have shrunk a little but she was obviously not one of those old grannies diminished in inches by age and osteoporosis; maybe plenty of milk and cheese had been her safeguard instead of HRT, Genna noted. (She had tried without success to persuade her mother to take this of late but her mother would have none of it, she hated visiting doctors.) The kettle was immediately filled from a nearby stone sink and preparations made for a cup of tea.

"Aye, It's been a long time, young Gen. What can I do for thee?"

"In a way, Mrs. Clarke, I don't want to intrude upon your privacy." Genna was hesitant. "On the other hand you may know things that could be really helpful."

"It's yon Gatenbys your after, I'll be bound. Tha's not from police? I want for telling them over much. Big lads they were - filled this room in their black ribbed jumpers draped with technical equipment. Not that they weren't polite, not like them newspaper men. They knew it all but still wanted to know about when I was in service at t'house."

Genna had a feeling the ground was being grabbed from under her feet by this tall, pin-neat old person and strove to regain her footing. "No, and I'm sorry, I'd no idea you'd been pestered. Please don't…." But Mrs. Clarke interrupted her.

"Aye, but thou's different, lass. I don't mind

chattin' to you - be nice over a cup a' tea, not like them damn reporters." She growled to herself as she went off to make the tea and left Genna in a fever of anticipation as to whether she was at last going to hear something positive about 'The Croft.'

She gazed around the small living room that seemed to go back in time to old black and white films she'd seen of the forties. The kitchen range was still there, no doubt the object of many black leadings. A cosy coal fire blazed in the grate. Lacy head covers on the back of two armchairs by the fire and a tab rug with its dark edges and diamond centre were obviously somebody's handy work from days gone by. Three wise monkeys sat on the high mantlepiece with their tiny paws over the appropriate bits, perhaps signifying Mrs. Clarke's philosophy, Genna mused - 'see all, hear all and say naught and if thee ever does ought for naught, do it for thee se'n' .

Genna sat by the velveteen covered table next to the window as Mrs. Clarke appeared with a tray holding tea things and a large plate of home-made ginger biscuits. Genna tried to take the tray off her but she brushed the help aside independently.

"Did this all my life in service 'till I were twenty and then some more for my Bert - he brought me here, he did and I stayed ever more. He's been gone since he were no'but a lad at sixty-five. On me own for over twenty years now."

"Good heavens! So you worked at 'The Croft' all the time before you were married?"

"Aye, between wars you might say. Emmy Gatenby were a young lass then."

"Just the three of them?"

"Madam, her husband and Emmy. Mr Gatenby were a lot older than his missus and bad with his chest. Used to clough something terrible - gassed in the 1914-18. Died when I was with them and he'd been in hospital a fair while then."

Genna made a mental note he could not have been the one under the ground; the police must have ruled him out.

"He never wanted to leave 'The Croft'. Ehh... it were a beautiful place then - a treat to see. Great sweeping lawns like they'd been cut with scissors and the beds and rockery full of flowers all spring and summer long. It were a paradise to set eyes on."

"So, the police asked you if you knew the identity of the body, I suppose?"

"They fished around it from every blessed angle. I've thought on it right often. Just get some more hot water and put me mind to it again."

Genna sighed. It looked as though it would be a fruitless visit, but the old lady appeared to be enjoying herself and did not hurry as she poured out more strong tea.

"When he died Madam turned to Emmy more. Emmy was quiet, not one for gadding about, 'cept on them hosses, she could ride like a fiend. Her mother was always trying to make her be more sedate. Later she was the same with t' car, mad as

a hatter at first. Her mother always expected to
hear she'd knocked over a few folk on her trips to
Kettlington. Her mother changed though, turned in
on herself like. Mind you, she were always a cold
fish. She had Emmy at home and she didn't want to
know about much else. No men friends or stuff like
that."

"Did Emmy have boy friends?"

"Not what you'd call walkin' out proper like. Her
mother had an elder sister, widowed long before
Madam and she had two lads who used to come
and stay in the holidays, gangly they were, growing
like weeds in their teens and Emmy was sweet on
one of them. Dead moony she was when they were
comin'. Couldn't get any sense out of her. I
remember her mother had to nag her like mad and
she was usually a biddable girl." Mrs. Clarke's eyes
wandered off into the past. "I wonder what
happened to them boys. Emmy must have been
going on seventeen when I last set eyes on her. I
left to marry my Bert and the war came."

"But what about any other relatives? Nobody's
turned up to claim the house as far as anybody
knows." Genna fingered the tatty old key case in
her pocket and wondered if it would be any good
asking Mrs. Clarke about it.

"You wouldn't believe that house." The old lady
looked into the distance. "It were a little palace
inside. Talkin' about it has brought it all to mind.,
what with its polished floors (I were reet proud of
them) and oak panelling and there were a grand

fireplace in the front hall. Mind you, Mr Gatenby spent most of his time int'Rose room once he started to be ill."

"Rose room?" Genna felt a prickly finger on her spine.

"Aye, had a window like a rose. He wanted to be out of the way of the women where he could turn his lungs inside out in peace - nobody could hear him cough there."

"Poor man... but how do you mean?"

"To tell the truth, I could never find it. Door were part of the panelling and it had no handle. They told me not to bother cleaning it any road because he didn't like his stuff moved. They never knew but I came across it once and peeped in." Mrs. Clarke' s voice sunk to a whisper.

The prickly finger trailed further down Genna's back as she pulled the key out of her pocket. "Look, Mrs. Clarke, do you think this may have opened the panelling door?"

Mrs. Clarke bent forward to look at the object Genna held in her hand. The key lay there with the open outline of metal at its head forming a distinctive shape.

"Why, of course, lass", she replied beaming at Genna, "there's the shape of one of them Tudor roses at the end."

Genna finished her tea without rushing and thanked Mrs. Clarke, hoping she would not ask where she found the key. She left the cottage knowing exactly what she would do next.

As she walked on into the village square the resolve that had been so firm began to waver. The establishment of Summers and Goldthorpe presented its property wares in a double fronted, Dickensian bow window. John Glendenning was the manager. She was sure he would be only to delighted to give them any information he had, even the key for a couple of hours if she dare ask him. She could then go with Issy to look at 'The Croft'.

It was now over ten days since the 'find' and police activity in Elvingdale had cooled considerably, on the surface anyway. Here, she told herself, was a chance to go for something in the same way Issy conducted her affairs.

She opened the door purposefully. The reception desk was manned by a girl with pale blue eyes spiked with dark blue mascara. Her face was surrounded by a curly mane of gingery blonde hair. She was obviously an 'oft cumden', as the villagers called strangers who had lived there for anything less than twenty years.

"Good afternoon. Can I help you?" The smile was papered on, the accent decidedly Scots, confirming Genna's first suspicions.

"Is Mr. Glenddening in, please?"

The pale eyes seemed to turn a fraction steely as the answer came. "Noo, I'm afraid he's out just now."

"Oh! I wonder if I could...? She hesitated and then stopped, becoming abruptly aware that this girl, for all her outward appearance, was hostile and the one she should really be asking the favour of was John himself. No, it doesn't matter, it'll keep until I see John." Did she imagine it, or was the look even cooler?

Genna turned to the door calling thank you over her shoulder. She did not see the small jutting chin and the flared nostrils glaring at her retreating back but she caught the gist of the conversation between Miss Lion mane and a voice from the inner office.

"Another one for the Glendenning adoration society, Eh, Lionie?"

"Written all over her silly face." A laugh came from the office as Genna slowly closed the door.

"She does na' ken what she's up against. She won't lay a finger on my John while I've got breath in my body." The lion's mane was tossed back and the blue chip eyes flashed icy fire as Genna looked back through the window.

She gave a shiver as she walked back down the street. A relationship with John was not going to be an easy ride for Issy after all, although it was not quite as hopeless as her quest for one with William.

When she was walking back past Bessie's cafe that particular set of emotions took a further setback. The place was empty and Bess waved a friendly arm from inside beckoning Genna in for a cup of tea.

"For heavens sake, sit down and take the weight off your feet for a minute." Bess put a cup in front of Genna and poured strong tea out of a metal pot. Genna reflected that if she went on like this, after Mrs. Clarke's offering, her insides would be turning tannin coloured.

"Thanks, Bessie, can't be too long, as much as I'd like to. I have to go to Kettlington with the school's minibus to pick up the kids."

"What about the news then?"

"What news?"

"Mean to say you don't know?" I thought Issy would have told you."

"I've no idea... What?"

"Young Farrington, got engaged to somebody called Debora Worthington. Who the heck's she when she's at home?"

Genna's mind seemed to collapse in on itself. Life turned to grey tinged dullness instead of being its earlier bright Technicolor. Her expression showed none of the feelings inside her as she looked back as Bess. "How did you...?" She began.

"Yorkshire Post this morning. 'The engagement is announced between Debora Anne Worthington of Salisbury, Wiltshire and Dr. William Farrington etc. etc." Bess waved the paper in the air. "I'm surprised Issy didn't mention it."

"I know Debora is a very dishy air-hostess. Issy thinks she's rubbish - not the right one for William and she certainly does not want her as a sister-in-law. Knowing Issy, she's probably trying to forget it ever happened."

"Well! What a state of affairs. Sorry I mentioned

it. What with that and the state of trade, there's no good news today."

"Customer numbers down?"

"Could be worse but not much. Foot and mouth's still got a lot to answer for. Never say die... we're all alive and kicking and ready to fight another day." She grinned at Genna who listened to the well worn phrases and felt ashamed as she shoved the image of Debora and William out of her mind.

Issy phoned full of woe and the news about William. "Father's taking us all out for a meal at 'The Strid' restaurant on Saturday to celebrate! Celebrate could you believe! Can't wait, that is until it's Sunday and I'm off for the day with John - it's keeping me alive."

"I hope you have a great time. I'll want to know the details, just don't forget what you said about attractive men." Genna kept quiet about the chatter she'd heard in the estate agents.

"Oh, what the hell! You know about gathering rosebuds - well 'Old time he is aflying and those sweet flowers that bloomed today, tomorrow could be dying' or something and I'm going to collect a damn great armful."

Genna smiled to herself at what a tonic Issy was for all her dedicated self interest. She came off the phone if not happy, at least aware that friends could be life enhancing.

When she thought about 'The Croft' she decided it maybe would have to wait. Issy had too much on her mind and the police in all probability would still be investigating. On the other had she could go and have a quiet sniff around by herself.

DIARY NOTES.
1939

Mr. Chamberlain has been unsuccessful in his attempt to avert conflict with Germany and on 3rd. September war was declared. I still cannot see it will affect my own life very much. Mother says that in the last war a lot of the poorer people actually starved in 1914 because they were not given rations but here in the Dales I do not believe that could happen.

Rory writes to me about how exciting his life is and how he loves the RAF. as he calls it. More importantly, he says if he has leave he will come and visit although it may be some time as he must see his mother too.

Tom also has joined the RAF although he has not written lately. Nobody seems to think that women will ever have any part in helping the war effort. I would certainly not like to fight but maybe I could learn to be a nurse. I do not expect they will let me but I could drive an ambulance. Mother says I am being ridiculous and I'd probably kill off more wounded than I saved.

Mother listens to the wireless endlessly. She says war is ghastly and before long there could be air-raids. They are expected quite soon. She thinks after what happened in the last war we will be given gas masks too. There are no signs of them yet. It is almost as though the rest of Great Britain is holding its breath waiting for something desperately awful to start. It's all a bit tedious.

CHAPTER SEVEN

Saturday brought a high, clear blue sky. Pale blossoms hung heavily on the trees in the village square, the occasional zephyr sending clouds of petals showering like confetti onto the cobbles.

From her bedroom window in the farm house Genna could see cars on the road in the distance on the side of the hill, telling her the village would be busy with tourists. The bar in 'The Unicorn' would be heaving all weekend if the weather held out. She hoped it would do just that for Issy's day out with John.

Her mother was at the sink in the kitchen washing and grading eggs as Genna looked for bread to toast.

"Does Pete want you today, Gen, or are you free?"

"I promised I would do a lunch-time session if the weather was good and then help with the busy time in the evening. He has taken on new help for when it warms up but they need watching to start with."

I thought you might take yourself off into Kettlington. Buy a new top, or something you fancy for a change with your bar money."

"I can't see I'll have that much time. I was going to come back home, grab a bite to eat and help dad but I'll see, Mum. Thanks for the thought." Genna pushed the bread under the oven grill and looked for some home-made marmarlade. The toaster had packed up some time ago; nobody had considered it worth mending and a new model was not on their shopping list. She opened the door to one of the big cupboards. Have we any cornflakes?"

"Your father finished them off." Genna made a mental note that they were probably not on the shopping list either, yet here was her mother encouraging Genna to spend money on new tops. She would not , she concluded, be temped by going into Kettlington this Saturday.

On leaving the farm she had pushed the Tudor rose key into her pocket thinking as she drove down the twisting lanes, whether they were really withholding evidence from the police as Issy had suggested. After all, it had not been found on the body but quite a few yards away. Was it just Issy doing the drama as was her habit?

It was three o'clock when the lunch time trade eased off and Genna left the pub. Should she, or shouldn't she? The question ran around her brain as she walked across the car park towards the old truck. She turned the key in the ignition. The engine gave a lurching grumble, reluctant to leap into life. "Oh, not you as well!" She muttered trying the key again. This time it managed to spark and flicker into life. She breathed a sigh of relief as she drove out of the car park.

She was not aware of making any conscious decision as she drove through the village and out past the church but somehow she was on her way to 'The Croft'.

The gate leading up the sloping drive to the house was open, slumped at an angle. The drive inclined ahead of her as she left the trees and hedges behind with their thick undergrowth and glanced towards the house.

Tall bay windows on either side of the frontage were boarded up between stone lintels but the grey stone looked solid, covered in parts by creepers making it look more attractive. Empty windows of upstairs rooms looked down watchfully under pointed eaves. where old nests could be seen, swifts or house martins, a lucky sign Genna knew.

The house was resting, waiting. The feeling was strong. Genna shivered not knowing whether it was for the good or bad.

Having driven the truck up to the front, she turned it around to point down the hill in case it would not start. The gravel was spread out in a wide circle but it was ill kept with long spikes of grass poking through its surface. The neat lawns Mrs. Clarke remembered were unkempt and disappeared into what was left of tangled flower beds.

Genna climbed out of the truck slowly and looked around cautiously. Tyre marks on the drive told of recent activity. A pathway leading down to the woods on the right appeared to be yellow-taped off. Genna knew it would lead to where they had dug to divert the stream and not far away through the wood would be 'The Rectory'. There was no

visible movement or sound except for bird song
and a breeze stirring the trees behind the house.

AUGUST 1940

*I find it difficult to believe I shall never see my two
cousins again. The love I have for them and the
things we shared are as strong as ever in my mind.
In reality the recipients of the love has gone, shot to
pieces in the skies over the English channel. I expect
the fact that both Rory and Tom already had some
flying hours put them straight into the thick of this
dreadful war. Tears of anger and grief spring to my
eyes whenever I think about it. I know I could have
married Rory if he had asked me.*

*I am going to try and keep some sort of dated
record, not just jotted notes, starting with the
death of my cousins in the Battle of Britain, so that
when I look back I will never forget the importance
of doing this, that is if I ever live to record it.*

*In the Spring of this year Churchill spoke of the
monstrous tyranny we are facing and the toil,
sweat and tears that could be ahead. We would
fight to our last breath and Great Britain was at the
start of one of the most deadly battles. From the
quiet of the Dales it seemed likely only words; now I
know the truth of it and somehow everything has
changed.*

*For the first time in my life I feel a great need for
some sort of revenge, revenge for Rory's death
particularly. I may be called up to join the services*

in the future but I am ready to volunteer now I am nineteen.

I am overwhelmed by the idea I could do something useful to fight back against this bestial Furher and his pack of Nazi animals. It will NOT be a non-fighting home front job as mother would want. (There will be a tussle over that.) I am going to volunteer for the Women's Auxiliary Air Force - a big decision but then I will be away from the safety of this place, maybe even in London in the war proper. I will feel as though I am doing something about their loss, even should it be menial work. I will be in the air force blue uniform like Rory and fighting for the same cause he died for.

Having made sure she was alone, Genna turned to go around the back of the house to see what that held. The drive led into a cobbled yard with stables and outbuildings, no doubt home to the horses and from where Emily started her wild riding. Another, better kept part, appeared to have been used as a garage.

The land and its wood sloped steeply upwards behind the stable yard giving shelter from the elements. Peeling paint spoke of the neglect the property had suffered.. The back entrance itself and what must be kitchen windows were covered in by a long, low porch with a slate roof. Flower pots with dry crumbling remains stood dejectedly on window ledges making the place look even more ramshackle.

The porch door was jammed open and Genna cautiously made her way towards it hoping to be able to see through the window into the kitchen. The rear door itself looked oak solid and tightly shut. She took the heavy key out of her pocket with no real thought of getting it open. Putting it in the lock she turned it with little effort. The door swung open leaving her standing in front of a dark interior and hardly able to believe what she had done, or it had been quite so simple.

Genna stood stock still trying to decide. Should she lock it up again and wait for Issy so that they could explore the house together, or...? After a moment's hesitation her curiosity got the upper hand and she stepped over the threshold. Maybe she would find a solution as to who was the occupant of the grave in the trees.

It was quite difficult to see in the dim light of the interior. A mushroom smell pervaded the atmosphere of what must have once been a large kitchen. A dirty stainless steel sink, an array of old fashioned wooden cupboards, not unlike those in their own farmhouse and a grubby looking gas stove, were all that remained of the fittings. There was lino on the floor, the pattern lost in dust and time.

A door opposite was obviously the way forward. Genna opened it gingerly. It led into a passage. She peered down its length to what must be the interior of the house. She made her way carefully into the gloom to where she could see light ahead.

The hall was the first revelation. There, a high ceiling to the upper part of the house towered into plastered glory and light, its immediate access being a wide staircase The parquet floor was a bit dull, long since untouched by Marion Clarke's deft hand but still beautiful. A large impressive open fireplace with stone blocks above it were curved into a smooth baronial arch dominating the whole.

The things that next caught Genna's eye were single Tudor roses carved here and there on the corners of the oak panelled walls. The panelling covered a large area and altogether there were numerous roses. Whoever had been responsible for old Mr. Gatenby's Rose room certainly knew the best way to lose a tree was in a forest, Genna noted as she went over to feel one of the carved roses. It was immoveable. As part of the panelling, a door without a handle would be difficult to find particularly as there was little light from the boarded up windows at the front of the house.

On further inspection there were two large rooms downstairs which held the bays either end of the house frontage. They had little to offer except large mahogany fireplaces but no panelling.

Back in the hall, Genna tried to remember Mrs. Clarke's exact words. Surely she mentioned the Rose room as though it were downstairs in the hall. Nothing had been said about upstairs, unless the room was... above the hall. Genna made for the stairs.

There was panelling up the first flight and around

the corner to the next, then a corridor, more panelling and Tudor roses. The dank smell of unused air made her desperate to fling open doors and windows letting in sunshine and breezes, reviving it from its dead state to being alive once more. She knew it was not possible. She was not supposed to be there never mind opening windows. She opened the door to the first bedroom, her footsteps clattering on the bare wood.

The room was empty, large and bare but the windows were not boarded. She went over to look out and was astounded at the panorama before her. The house occupying high ground, looked down over the drive, the tree tops, the road to the church and the village beyond. Further left over the wood, she saw 'The Rectory' and its drive. Surely Emily Gatenby must have stood there and gazed at that same scene just as she herself was doing at that very moment. She shivered.

She left the view and tried doors on the opposite side of the corridor but the rooms were smaller and again held nothing of interest.

There was a large antiquated Victorian bathroom, the sort that had just come back into fashion. She closed the door on that and looked back down the corridor, deciding she would have a quick look in what must be the other front bedroom.

Opening the door it appeared to be quite empty with a similar view to the first but then something on the floor in the corner of the room caught her eye. She moved cautiously into the room and bent to pick up the 'thing'. Holding it between her fingers she realised it was a faded, once pink bed sock, like a baby's knitted bootee only in adult size. The wool was pilled from where its owner's foot had rubbed against the bedclothes. Surely this must have been Emily Gatenby's room and possibly where she had been found dead by Dr. Farrington. There was a strong feeling Emily was close, her ghost in the room watching her.

Genna shuddered still holding the object as some small sound caught her ear. She looked quickly towards the door. An unknown hand pushed it slowly open making it creak menacingly. A shadow lengthened, a precursor of something or somebody. Genna froze seeing the spectre of her nightmare coming through the doorway holding out the key to her. The skull grinned, sinister, horrendous. The spectre was razor sharp, holding the centre stage of her consciousness but not in reality; even so she shrieked in terror, dropped the bed sock, and shutting her eyes to block out the revulsion of what she might see, charged across the room and out of the door.

She remembered little about leaving the house except stopping determinedly to lock the back door behind her. She leaned against the porch to catch her breath and calm her pounding heart.

Heading for the safety of the truck, common sense began to assert itself. Just because she hadn't thought of that stupid dream for ages it had crept up on her unawares when some movement of air, probably from the kitchen, had opened. the bedroom door. She smiled to herself and looked back at 'The croft'. It had certainly played its own tricks on her.

As she looked something made her turn completely and stare. Between the big windows of the upstairs rooms there was a long gap, covered in half grown and old creeper. Mostly hidden by the growth there appeared to be another window, dirty and almost camouflaged into the background. Surely it was a round window, a Tudor rose shaped window? Genna knew it belong to neither of front upstairs rooms but, more curiously, there had been no door between them - no obvious door but maybe a door she had missed because it had no handle. It would be directly above the hall and what else could it be but Mr. Gatenby's retreat? She felt a surge of elation and success.

She hesitated, urging herself to go back and look for the door, then shook her head, There was no way on earth she could make herself do it. The spectre, imaginary or not, had been too real. She would tell Issy and together they would come and find what she assumed others who had cleared the house may well have missed, namely The Rose room.

CHAPTER EIGHT

Genna looked around the busy bar where Pete and two more girls, younger than herself, were serving. Saturday night had been lively but now the pub was doing a roaring trade at its Sunday lunch time opening.

Walkers were plentiful, looking determined and vocal about it, booted and anoraked with sticks and knapsacks abounding. The wide, blue sky and the draw of the Dales had worked their spell.

Genna had been up with the birds helping her father clean the shippens where they usually kept a few cows, largely to supply the farm with milk and cheese. In no way did they profess to be dairy farmers.

Over the noise and general hubbub around her Genna just managed to hear the telephone trill out at the back of the bar. There was a constant stream of customers calling orders while she pulled pints; arm straining work but something at which she was competent.

She pushed the thick dark hair out of the way in an impatient gesture and looked round for Pete. He had disappeared. She scolded him under her breath. She completed the order with good grace and gave the customer change while the telephone persisted. She really had to answer it. The Fell Rescue team may be contacted through the pub as Pete was one of its mainstays. There was no telling when some inexpert soul could take a step too far on a slippery path too high.

"The Unicorn Inn."

"Genna?"

"Hi, John?" She thought she recognised John Glendenning's voice but it had a urgent, hard tone to it and the line croaked making it impossible to hear for a moment.

"What's the problem, John?"

"I'm on the mobile at Hebgarthdale…. Issy's had an accident… chasing after Fifi …there was an old mine shaft…" The mobile began to break up again and Genna cursed.

"Terrible reception, John.. What do you want me to do? Shall I get Pete?"

"More to the point is his rock climbing stuff there?" The line cleared as quickly as it had broken up.

"It's in his Range Rover, parked at the back of the pub. I saw it earlier this morning. Is issy OK?"

I've got a rope around her but she's stuck down the shaft. Listen, I'm going to ring William. I'll get him to come over and pick up the equipment. I can manage to get her up with a sling and a pulley if William helps me. I expect he's having a lie in with Debora."

"Shall I call the Fell Rescue out as well?" Genna pushed out of her mind the comments about Debora.

"No, it's not necessary. If Pete comes that's fine but if he's busy we'll manage well enough between the two of us. William will have his medical kit for emergencies."

"Right, John. Tell William exactly where you are and it may be possible to drive part way if it's off the road by the Hebgarthdale signpost.

"True, you mean go along the valley bottom and save time. That's great I'll get William going as soon as I can."

"Good luck, John." Genna hung up the phone and heaved a deep breath. Poor Issy, rushing after Fifi and not looking where she was going sounded so like her. She looked around the bar. Where was Pete? She turned to one of the girls helping. "Seen Pete anywhere?"

"He's down the cellar changing a barrel."

"Heck! I suppose I'll have to go and get him. Can you manage here?"

"Sure. The best of British." The girl grinned and nodded.

Genna knew only to well what she was implying. Being down the dark cellar alone with Pete had its own set of hazards especially if he was feeling frisky.

The cellar steps were steep as she went carefully down calling Pete as she went.

The light was quite bright at the bottom but further along the barrels became darker until she could hardly see. "Pete, there's a call for you...PETE … AHHHhhhh!... Genna shrieked as large muscular arms grabbed her from behind and a whiff of aftershave caught her intake of breath.

"Patients rewarded at last! I knew you'd come

looking for me down here one of these days."
Pete's voice growled with mock ferocity into her
ear as he pretended to bite it. His beard ticked as
he turned.

"You great animal! GET OFF!" Genna gasped as
he chuckled and growled into her other ear.
"LISTEN for heavens sake, IT'S IMPORTANT!" She
yelled at him.

Pete stopped his gorilla antics and turned her in
his arms, making the most of the physical contact
as he did so. She wished he did not feel good but
she had urgent things to see to and it would be
fatal to flirt and encourage him.

"Is it business?" He wanted to know as she
pushed him away.

"Of course... business, why else would I come
down here?"

"I thought maybe...OK, let's have it then." He
stepped away from her back to the barrels and
listened carefully enough to the tale of Issy's plight.

"John needs the pulleys, harness and sling
equipment to get Issy out. I told him you had that
in the Range Rover. William's going to come over
and get it, if that's okay. But... if you could just take
the Range Rover up there it would be quicker and
you could get closer."

"Umm, no real problem but I'm pushed to come
at the moment. This barrel has to be changed and
there's a pub full of customers upstairs... only those
two young 'uns to cope" Pete scratched his beard
but there was little indecision. "Look, you've driven

the Range Rover before, take it up there with
William. There's all the equipment they'll need. I've
been through it lately, what's more young
Glendenning's a paid up member when it comes to
rescue - I've seen him in action. The lass alright, is
she, he's got a rope on her?"

"That's what he said and I'll get back as soon as I
can."

Pete turned and gripped her arm, looking at her
with mild severity on his craggy features. "Listen,
Flower, don't worry about rushing... just ring me if
there are ANY problems - ANY AT ALL. My mobile's
there. Don't mess about."

"Thanks for that, Pete, I won't." She nodded and
shot him a grateful look as she disappeared up the
cellar steps, eager to be of use in Issy's rescue and
hoping against hope that Debora had not decided
to come along for the ride with William.

DIARY NOTES
November, 1940:

*Some little time after war was declared mother
was approached to take evacuees. She was quite
panic stricken at the thought and did her best to
dodge it. A strangely quiet brother and sister
arrived, very pale and cockney, mesmerised by
anything to do with grass and trees! They had lived
in back to backs and didn't know about lawns.
Mother is trying to be kind to them but they do not
look very happy. I don't think they feel safe with the*

open spaces away from their street life.

I have seen very little of this. After a big fight with mother my life has undertaken a vast change on account of joining the WAAF. The uniform is ill-fitting and uncomfortable but it makes me feel close to Rory and I keep his letter secure in my top pocket.

When I first came here I hated this place with its flat Lincolnshire countryside, after being used to the Yorkshire Dales all my life. There are cold huts with their bare boards in which we are housed and hard narrow beds to sleep in.

I do not mind the uniform, or for that matter the drilling; 'Yes, Sir, No, Sir, Up Your Nose, Sir'. No worse than mother! The work is, as I expected, menial, cleaning, scrubbing and preparing vegetables so far. I hope to make use of the fact I can drive and will apply for a transfer in that direction but it won't be easy, they actually believe women are incapable of anything technical.

The discipline and structure of the days are east to accept, the thing I find so dreadfully hard to bear is the usual lack of privacy. My life is totally invaded by other women. I did not think of myself as a snob but some of their habits are disgusting; the way they eat and the cheap stuff they put on their faces. I don't find it easy to understand what some of them are saying even. Fortunately they are not all the same. In some ways I feel like I did at boarding school and so, of course, have employed the same tactics against it - I keep very quiet. They give up on me after a while and I get Empty Emmy or Silent Sally for nick names behind my back. Slowly they have accepted I am not bad but do not join in with any degree of ease.

I have brought all the books I could manage but that is the other thing I hate, I can never read when I want.

Bombing began in earnest this summer, key targets, dockyards, factories, airfields, horrible casualties, then in September, the blitz on London. We have been hit twice but not badly, there were no actual fatalities. Some idiots who left it too late to take cover were hit by shrapnel and took some nasty jags.

Death could be peeping around every corner but there is a vital excitement in trying to elude it so that in a strange way one tolerates the unpleasant habits of ones fellows and comes to realise it has brought us all closer together in bonds of friendship I have never experienced before.

The truth of what happened at Dunkirk is still in our minds. Four days from 30th May, little boats brought men back home from French beaches or ferried them to larger craft and returned for more. Many were so lucky but others, probably thousands, were not - It is so dreadful I cried at the thought.

The fact to face was that German troops could cross that slim band of water in their hundreds at any minute and the country would be under Gestapo rule, jack boots, 'HEIL HITLER' and submission. That must be the most terrifying thought.

Genna ran across the car park with the Range Rover keys as William's estate car arrived. He was alone and despite all the anxiety over Issy and the situation with his engagement, Genna's spirits lifted at the prospect of having him to herself.

Having explained about Pete's decision and helped William to transfer the medical paraphernalia from his car, they were quickly under way. "Did John tell you any more about Issy? Was she hurt?" Genna asked as she took the big vehicle through its gears and drove out of the village, winding upwards over the hill.

"She seems to have hurt her leg, he didn't know how badly. They were walking the moor top over Hebgarthdale and talking about disused lead mines where the old shafts in that area are protected. Fifi ran off and knowing how clumsy she can be, Issy ran after her, over a rise and disappeared. John had my mobile number and he's telling me this as I dragged on clothes and fired questions at him."

"How awful for John! I expect he feels responsible."

"Issy could do with a permanent minder, bless her." William shoved fingers through his blond hair in a sign of tension so far not obvious. "Anyway, the shaft was covered with rotten planking - she went through it. Fortunately the subsidence had tilted it a bit and she grabbed at some sort of spindly growth on the way down and a semi-permanent obstacle stopped her from going the whole distance, probably more rotten planking."

Genna had a shock horror vision of Issy losing her footing and injuring herself or worse as she tumbled further down into the blackness of the mine shaft.

"John thanked his lucky stars he had a length of rope clipped to the underside of his knapsack from his last trip. He managed to get a bowline down. Issy was scared to death to move in case her foothold and grip gave way but he talked her through it and she got it on okay."

"A bowline?" Genna queried.

"A bowline is a knot made next to a loop. The rope to the knot tightens the loop if you pull on it. I've never tried it but I know it works. John's the expert, thank God!"

Genna glanced at the man sitting reassuringly beside her, his arm along the back of the seat as she drove. He looked relaxed in a striped rugby shirt but she knew he must be anything but and hoped she looked as cool. "She certainly chose the best companion to rescue her. "What about Fifi?"

"Looking down the shaft, barking! They're two for a pair. Life's always been one adventure after another for our Isso. She has a habit of coming out at the other side waving a lettuce leaf and saying how very slimming it's all been!"

Genna laughed unaffectedly despite her anxiety. That was Issy all over but she knew really they

were shoring up the worries they both harboured
as she drove as fast as she dared up to the
Hebgarthdale signpost.

The 'pull off' overlooking the dale gave a
magnificent view. John's Merc was parked there
already. A wide open pathway led down into the
valley bottom and it proved a fairly simple
operation to drive into the immense dale after a
few initial bumps.

The dale was bordered on one side by tall castles
of vast limestone escarpments heading towards
the sky. On the other side the land sloped upwards
towards the flatter moor top which was apparently
was where John and Issy were heading.

As she drove Genna tried not to think about Issy
and the awful sense of claustrophobia she must be
feeling as the mine shaft closed over her while she
clung onto the rope. She thought of William and
wished their errand was not so fraught and they
had a different sort of relationship. Did it show in
her eyes, this wealth of feeling she had for him?
She could end up looking a fool if she did not keep
it under wraps.

Even so she felt there was some understanding
between them, a chemistry of sorts of which they
were both aware. It was not just admiration for
Issy's big brother, she could not pinpoint the
feeling but it was real enough.

She negotiated the rough parts of their chosen
path well, able to use the power of the vehicle and

with no qualms about her ability to do so. Taking a rickety old truck over farm land made this seem like a stroll in the park.

William broke the silence as he pointed ahead. "You see that ridge towards the end of the valley? John waiting up there. He's hoping to spot us and help carry equipment."

Genna found herself driving faster, bumping and jolting over the flat valley floor as they drove nearer to Issy's predicament. "I don't think we'll be able to take the Range Rover far up that slope. Maybe Pete would but it could end up damaging something and not getting Issy back." She glanced up and saw a figure dwarfed on the horizon by the ridge, arms signalling. "Look, William, there's John," she pointed.

Turning the wheel towards the slope she drove as far as she dared until rocks and uneven ground prevented progress. The pair got out quickly and began to unload the emergency equipment. It was not long before they saw John running down towards them.

CHAPTER NINE

Carrying the equipment up the hill to the flat moorland above did not prove too difficult a task when it was distributed between the three of them. Genna could see a stubby hawthorn around which John had secured a rope obviously not far from the shaft. Fifi was also tied to the tree to prevent her getting into mischief. John went to check on Issy then came back to them.

"Issy says her leg has stiffened up; it's hurting like hell and she doesn't know how she's going to get into the harness. I think one of us is going to have to go down and help her. She sounds quite distressed." John was trying hard not to look uneasy.

"You two men can heave me up and down more easily that if one of you goes down." Genna did not hesitate to volunteer. William looked at John who nodded at the obvious sense of the idea.

"Quite sure you're happy with that, Genna?" William's hand on her shoulder prompted a positive reply.

"No problem, just show me what to do."

First a firm, strong base had to be found to take the pulley. Rope was now plentiful and as the two worked together with Genna as a willing dogsbody, the rescue clicked into gear.

Once Genna was into the harness and they had ensured it was fastened securely around her, they checked the pulley and its ropes were in place with the karabines.

She was glad she had worn jeans and T shirt to work in the pub, a skirt would have been a distinct problem.

John showed her how to fasten the crash helmet. He appeared to be well versed from training and experience in rock climbing and rescue as he did the job quickly and efficiently with William's help.

Genna had a torch but the blackness of the shaft was intimidating as she was lowered into it. What madness had made her volunteer to do this? There was a smell of damp fungus that she could almost taste. Water dripped into some subterranean depth and with the slight tilt in the land had collected in parts to supply life to foliage in stunted tufts. The vegetation poked out from the sides and was no doubt what Issy had endeavoured to grab in a bid to break her tumble down the shaft.

"Nearly there, Issy ,"she called as she pointed the light below to try and catch a glimpse of Issy's position. She spidered down another few feet and could see Issy's bulk scrunched up against the side of the shaft.

"Genna... go slowly... I daren't breathe... this lot could give way."

Genna caught the muffled voice that drifted up to her as she drew nearer and began to understand how scared the girl below her must be. She herself had a life insurance harness, all Issy had was an unstable foothold and a single rope cutting into her.

Genna looked upwards to a small hole of light and John and William at the top, The claustrophobia she had feared Issy would have overtook her; the earth was closing over her head, she was trapped as though in a coffin, buried alive. She steered her thoughts firmly to another route, to the task in hand and, as she almost drew level with Issy, flashed the torch upwards to let John know.

"Issy, soon have you out. Where does your leg hurt?" Genna could see as she shone the torch, just how precarious was Issy's position. One hand was gripping some small spindly growth and both her feet covered a tiny ledge of rotten planking sticking out from the side of the shaft. She was covered in mud and her face had a bright red flag of graze down one side.

"Genna, it's awful... my knee I can't bend it... probably a torn ligament." She shifted her position a fraction and small stones cascaded, diving to the depths below, suspended in space for what seemed an age before a faint splash echoed back. Issy groaned with fear and pain. Genna knew she had to get the harness on her quickly but how to manage it she had no idea.

"Issy, listen, we've got to do this harness. I'm going to be right beside you. You must trust me and hold on to me so you can't fall." Genna's strength was showing through.

The next minutes were hours as Genna cajoled and coaxed Issy into the harness. Issy moaned in agony trying to bend her knee as Genna sympathised and encouraged. Her eyes had become accustomed to the light and she could see how white and tortured was Issy's expression. Bruises on her face had begun to swell and she looked like a boxer on the losing end of a bloody fight.

When at last the weight of her body was supported by the harness and its ropes, Issy shifted her weight and the planking broke away from underneath them. It crashed down banging the sides of the shaft with the debris it disturbed, until again it splashed eerily to the bottom of he shaft.

Issy gave a small shriek and whimpered with fear as she clung onto Genna, who could well imagine that catastrophe might grab its second chance, a chance she was not going to allow.

"It's okay, Issy, you can't fall, you're safe in that harness." Genna comforted her until she was quiet.

The harness in place, Genna unclipped the pulley ropes and swapped them over to Issy leaving herself on her own safety line. She knew she would have to wait until Issy was out before following her, not a prospect she relished at all but at least she was safe. She signalled to John and William to start Issy's ascent, then as Issy grew smaller and smaller, Genna turned off the torch and kept still engulfed by the dim light, the drips and the smell.

DIARY NOTES

Spring, 1941

The bombing in the latter half of last year was fearful; so many died in air raids and fires. Here there were often girls sobbing quietly for somebody they'd lost. General Rommel has now arrived in Tripoli and all our encouraging gains in North Africa have been lost.

It is not clear how we are going to win through, or what will become of us if we lose. They say our men folk would be taken away to be used as slave labour, no doubt a worse fate would await women. We would be dragged of the face of the earth as a nation, that is the terrible part .

We just know we have to fight to the death and there is a tremendous spirit of determination amongst all the girls around me. We are totally united in the thought that we are not going to let the Germans batter this island to death. You see I am different from how I was before.

I am doing a course in motor transport. It is SUPER. I can drive already so I have a big advantage over some girls. I am learning all about the internal combustion engine. I can change wheels, even on a three ton truck!

I believe I am actually getting better at talking to people - just better, not good but I have been trying. It is so different not having mother here. I actually miss her and I write often but I realise now how isolated my life was at home. I became worse when father died with mother standing back from things and taking me with her. I feel part of the world here. Although some of it is good, at other times it is a dreadful place.

*This April I have been taking a special driving test and I have passed with flying colours. I will be able to drive lorries and ambulances as well as staff cars. What an achievement! At the moment I am ferrying laundry! It will all change as they are beginning to realise how useful and **really capable** women are. Soon I will be able to drive Officers, even maybe Top Brass!*

At last the pulley rope was sent back down and Genna was able to make the ascent to freedom and light once more. She heaved herself up over the edge as William helped her up and to her feet. She clung to him for a brief moment and he held her close, arms around her shoulders. He felt gloriously warm and comforting after the cold damp of the last half hour.

"Genna, that was so brave of you."

"Needs must...How's Issy?"

"I've given her a shot. John's doing the TLC bit with some hot sweet coffee from their picnic." He looked towards the pair. Issy was lying by the Hawthorn with Fifi beside her, licking wherever she could find to lick while John administered the hot drink. "She's improving by the minute...getting stroppy soon, I expect. I'll have to have a go at cutting those jeans off her injured leg, maybe splint it. She won't like that." William smiled down at her.

"But how's the heroine of the day, you okay?"

"Not exactly the Ritz down there," she smiled, "but I'm fine."

Issy did not look quite the recovered patient William had described, battered and bedraggled, Genna thought but she sounded much more like her usual self.

"Genna! Oh God! What a wimp I was. What would I have done without you?" She flung out her arms to Genna then grimaced as she moved her knee too quickly.

"For heaven's sake, Issy, keep still" William scolded as Genna went to hug her cautiously. "Don't want more damage done before I have a proper look at that knee."

"It's not a fracture, William, probably a tear at the top of the ligament."

The two carried on a medical discussion too technical for Genna but which culminated with Issy trying to dissuade William from cutting off the leg of her jeans. At the same time he cleaned up the graze on her face while she dodged his hand and squirmed at the pain. Genna exchanged glances with John, busy with equipment. Things were almost back to normal.

Issy's diagnosis had proved to be right - no fracture and William had been persuaded to examine her without a debag. Genna could see how the pain and shock were beginning to zap Issy's bravado.

"An inflatable splint will do the trick until we get

you back for an x-ray." William told his sister, head down at her level. "You'll be good as new in no time, Isso, back at home in one piece," he murmured comfortingly to her, obviously taking in what Genna had noticed. Issy nodded, accepting his reassurance.

Everything was taken down the hill and packed into the Range Rover. Issy was loaded along with the equipment so she was able to keep her splinted leg in position. She looked happier with John squashed beside her holding her hand until they arrived back at his car. Genna drove carefully while William kept a weather eye on the patient.

The rescue team headed for the pub to drop off Genna then sped on to Kettlington hospital for further investigations to Issy's leg.

It was well past five o'clock and things looked quieter at 'The Unicorn'. Genna would find Pete, tell him of their result and maybe arrange to come back later. She remembered she had not congratulated William on his engagement and wondered how Debora felt being left for the greater part of the day.

The other matter of the rose key had also been pushed to one side by more death-flouting matters. As soon as Issy was able to cope Genna would speak to her and decide what they should do.

It was when she arrived home with a sense of being mentally rather than physically tired that another worrying situation arose. Jose McFaiden was lying on the old sofa in the kitchen drinking a cup of tea, which Genna knew, was something as unlikely to happen as hens going for a swim.. Her mother's colour was never high but now she looked sallow and ill.

"Just skiving for a bit." She smiled at Genna as though everything in the world was just fine.

"Oh yes." Genna believed it not at all and reflected that in her response.

"All right then. Maybe I was a little too enthusiastic about the kitchen garden - felt a bit dizzy bending down. For heaven's sake don't look so ferocious, Genna."

Genna turned to the teapot, poured a cup of tea and sat down near her mother. Jose McFaiden could not be regarded as a typical farmer's wife. The rosey cheeked, sturdy specimens who were strong and usually well versed in the ways of animals were far removed from her slight, sensitive mother. Like Genna, she was well read, had been able to grasp Pythagoras and logarithms easily at school and could have had a reasonable conversation about Greeks and Romans with any historian.

Genna knew her father had been and was still a handsome man with his even features and winning smile and that he had never tried to hide his passion for farming. He had taken Jose along with him. She loved him, sometimes with impatience but was always loyal and helpful with his endeavours.

Her mother had quickly picked up the essentials of farm life as well as doing the office work and balancing the books but Genna never saw her as a farmer's wife in the true sense.

"Anyway, Genna, I've got plenty of stuff bedded out, lettuce carrots, beans, beets...you name it, so we won't starve this summer. You look a bit grubby. How was your day?"

"You may well ask." Genna drank the tea, and smiling to herself, began to tell her mother all about Issy's trauma. William coped so well, I think he's going to be a good doctor for the village practice," she finished. As an afterthought she continued. "Mother, why not make an appointment, see him, or his father and have a checkup."

"Don't be ridiculous, I'm fine." her mother made as though to get up but the dizziness or whatever, seemed to have persisted and she sank back again, trying to make it obvious there was nothing wrong. "You know very well I don't like doctors messed about with me and being asked intimate questions."

Genna did know this only too well. She had a strange attitude towards gypsies as well. The very mention of them made her mother's hackles rise. She must remember to question her father what that was all about.

CHAPTER TEN

Issy's plight soon saw her on the phone to Genna the following week. Genna noted at least she had been thoughtful enough to phone the bar at 'The Unicorn' at the early time and Genna was glad of the chance to talk to her.

"Total sum so far is three doctors, counting William and father, one orthopaedic surgeon, X-rays and a scan. It all boils down to the same thing - leg in plaster and immobilised for SIX weeks - my God! I shall be clean doolally by then."

"But, Issy, at least it's not broken." Genna felt sympathetic but almost wished she could be immobilised for six weeks.

"No - torn tendon at the top of my knee, like an Achilles at the back of your heel. they could do a synthetic repair but this guy thinks if I stay off it for six weeks it will mend itself. SIX WEEKS…. In plaster from my ankle to the top of my thigh and I can't drive …I can't get in the car."

"How's the rest of you?" Genna chuckled, hoping to make light of things.

"Yes, well, I shan't mind not going out for a bit, my face is such a mess and there are Technicolor bruises in some funny places. Genna, you must visit and save my sanity."

"Yes, I will… there are secret things I have to ask you about. I have to go now, customers… but let's think when we can manage it."

In a sheltered area on the leeward side of the

farmhouse there had once been an orchard of sorts
where pigs had been kept; now a few old fruit trees
remained. It was an area where daffodils grew in
the grass under the trees. A bench was placed to
view the magnificent expanse of the valley below.
There were no pigs on the farm now. Swill was not
allowed, which made them uneconomical, a fact of
great sorrow to Genna's father who loved the
round intelligent animals. The daffodils however,
thrived and it was their abundance that let Genna
on an errand which proved significant that
particular week.

"Gen, pop these in at the church when you're in
the village. There are so many of them. It's nice if
more people enjoy them." Her mother had
presented her with an armful of daffodils and
Genna had made a note to drop them off after
driving the school minibus into Kettlington.

It was when she was coming out of the church
and turning the truck round in the lay-by beside it,
that she saw a figure and sheep dog walking up the
road that let to 'The Croft'. It was Geoff Cordingly
of milk delivery fame with Wellingtons and a stick
looking as though he meant business.   She waited
while he drew near.

"Mornin, Genna. Pretty fair today." He stopped
and looked round as though to confirm the
statement.

"Not bad, Geoff. Going far?"

"Ah, well, away down memory lane y'might say."

Genna frowned, wondering what the old man

was talking about. He had been a resident of Elvindale for ever. She knew there was talk of his elder son planning to take over the milk round but it was, she realised, quite unusual to see him walking so purposefully out of the village and not driving his float.

"I hope they are good memories." It was not a question but it could have been.

"Not right sure. That's it y'see ...can't quite get it."

Genna was tempted to leave him to sort out his perverse memories but somehow, as he stood there pushing back his cap and shaking his head, she was spurred on to enquire further. "What is it to do with? Is it something special?" She frowned. He could tell her to mind her own business she reflected but he didn't.

"Nowt special but I'll tell you if you've a mind to listen." He sat down on a grassy bank beneath the wall.

Genna put out a hand to stroke his silky sheep dog as she went to sit down beside him wondering what was coming next.

"Eh, I'm right stiff these days, talk about schrematics. Wasn't like that all them years ago, after the war. Used to deliver milk up to 'The Croft' then with me dad. One of them teenagers I was, short back and sides brainwashed to say please and thank you properly, not like them grunts y'get now from young 'uns."

Genna's curiosity took on a new life - this was

going to be about 'The Croft'."I've heard folk say it used to be nice up there."

"Oh aye, it were beautiful. Them two women were a right funny pair though, never so much as gave you time of day. That's it though, police were nattering at me for what could I remember with taking milk there, or rather who I could remember being there. I couldn't remember nowt, could I, until later and I began to think on it."

"What DID you remember?" Now Genna was dying to know.

"There was something right odd to do wit porch at the back and I'm buggered if I kin think what it was and that's why I'm off up there to have a bit of a poke round. See if I kin stir me brains. Been drivin' me silly it has. Mind you it's a bit late to be telling' bobbies now."

"You never know, it may be vital." Genna stuck out her hand to help the old man up from the grass as he got his balance.

"Shouldn't think so. Don't hold y'breath, as my lads say." He chuckled and smiled at Genna. "Thanks, lass. Be seein' you."

A wet afternoon saw Genna off to 'the Rectory' for tea with Issy. She would have to walk from the village, the truck was playing up again.

Genna had spoken to Issy's mother and Marjorie Farrington had told her to come straight in as she herself would be out helping at a W.I. Whist drive.

Issy was lying on the velvety sofa in the sitting

room, the plastered leg stretched out along its length with Fifi as guardian beside it, (whilst there was nobody looking).

A cheerful fire was in contrast to the view from the window seat in the bay; trees could be seen thrashed by the wind and driving rain pelted against the long panes.

Genna's cheeks were bright and red, her dark hair pushed under the hood of the old blue anorak, rain soaked with walking from the village.

"Genna! Salvation at last. I'm going nuts with my own company..." then as an afterthought. "You must have been out in the rain." Typically Issy, when Genna looked half drowned.

"That blessed truck again. Where can I put these to dry?"

"In the kitchen, over the Aga rail. Stick the kettle on while you're there."

"Your face is healing quickly." Genna commented on her return from the kitchen as the two settled down to talk.

"Still sore from the bruising but my appetite is the worst thing. I'm bored out of my skull and constantly looking for food." Issy threw her hands in the air and the dog looked up with a dismayed expression at having her position disturbed. "Fifi and I are very grateful for each others company but things can be overdone." Fifi turned away with a 'disgusted from Tunbridge Wells' look.

"What the hell, Issy, you ARE ALIVE and pretty well - you'll soon be mobile and shedding inches by the minute. John has an excuse to dance attendance, so why not lie back and enjoy the rest?" Genna did not add that she would love it, preferably should she be in Kettlington library to wallow in books.

"You mean like if rape is inevitable." Issy managed a smile."

"Confusious knew a thing or two."

"Listen, I have stuff to tell you. First of all, remember we were off to the Strid Restaurant to celebrate William's engagement the night before this happened? Well who should arrive but John... opened the door for an apparition called Leonie with glittering blonde curly hair. No kid, my heart sank! He told me quite convincingly it was Summers and Goldthorpe's belated Christmas 'do' and there was a party of about eight of them there...so fair enough."

"Yes, I've seen her in the shop." Genna left out the rest.

"But he told me such a tale later when I bumped into him going to the loo. He'd seen Debora with us and wanted to know what she was doing there...he could hardly believe it when I told him."

Genna's attention focused at the mention of William.

"John said ...mind you, I had to drag it out of him, he'd seen her lately in a Chinese restaurant in Leeds and she was with this bloke. John recognised the guy, he's called Ian Sykes and he's a photographer who did some art work pictures in connection with a property John dealt with. Debora was all over him like a rash, like he was a lover, big time. Would you believe it?"

"Heavens! What do you make of that then?" Genna's heart was pounding and she didn't know whether to laugh or cry for William.

"God knows, I don't. I daren't confront William with it anyway. Maybe she's two timing him. But that's not all, apparently she blasted William out after Sunday for leaving her to spend the day by herself. All in all the course of true love is a fair old skid alley for those two!" Issy grinned wickedly. "Watch this space."

"How are things progressing with John?"

"Well we did try it the other night but with all the activity his willie caught on the edge of the plaster. He screamed and retired wounded." Issy doubled up with laughter and Genna joined in marvelling at Issy's uninhibited nature.

"I'd better go and make some tea, then I'll tell you my bit of news." Genna winked mysteriously as she left the room, feeling elated by the prospect of William's engagement being scuppered and then ashamed at such a response.

DIARY NOTES
December, 1941.

The Japanese have attacked the U.S. naval base at Pearl Harbour, Hawaii and the Americans are in the war. Churchill thinks this will save us. The girls think it will be marvellous: Yanks over here in droves.

I have found something I really like doing - I am officially a driver. I have the most extraordinary man to look after. He is quite a braided officer, (no names, no pack drill), but he is a real Casanova - large curling moustache and hands to match!

Apart from the official driving, my officer gets me to drop him off at the village pub where he spends the night with some floosie and then I have to pick him up first thing in the morning! He does not intend to miss out on anything. Well, perhaps he's right; any of us could go for a Burton at any old time; although I sometimes think the war was made for his sort and he'll live to be ninety.

He realises I'm not a talker and he thinks I'm very efficient and does not try any nonsense. Isn't it quite amazing? Mother would be horrified. I haven't told her too much about him in my letters!

SPRING 1942.

The Americans give out stockings and food we cannot otherwise get our hands on. They also seduce the girls with their easy friendliness and sexy manners. They smoke like bonfires and dance like maniacs - hops in the village hall will never be the same again. I can see how the other girls find them exciting but how it gets the backs up of our soldiers. I suppose their attraction has passed me by, they are not really my sort and now I feel so useful in the war.

After the tea had been poured Issy settled back as Genna recounted her trip to 'The Croft', the bed sock find and how she had fled the house then spotted the Rose room window.

"Don't you dare visit again until I can come with you. I just can't wait to see it."

"Hang on a minute, there's more." Genna replied. The next part concerning Geoff Cordingly's lapse of memory, gave Issy even more room for excited speculation and an in-depth discussion of the identity of the bones soon took over.

The thing is, old Mrs. Clarke said there were no men in Emmy's life except for her cousins who only arrived now and them. The guy we uncovered had to be somebody buried there secretly; he wasn't digging a tunnel now, was he?" Genna put common sense first.

"OK, have you got other ideas, go on - I can't wait to hear."

"Age-wise points to some secret boyfriend of Emmy's, maybe the enemy, either a spy, escaped prisoner, or even an airman and, last but not least, a toy boy of her mother's!"

"That sounds a bit unlikely." Issy chuckled. I thought Marion Clarke said Emmy's mother was a sourpuss."

"Mmm...maybe a passionate sourpuss? BUT nobody knew he was there, that smacks of guilt attached to him somewhere."

"But if we imagine he was some stray member of

the Luftwaffe who'd lost his wings and his way and
they'd rubbed him out, by whatever method, they
would have been keen to shout it around and
everybody would have known, surely, Genna?"

"Not if first of all, they'd hidden him and he'd
been in bed with one of them."

"Or even with BOTH OF THEM! They'd found out
about each other and..."

Gordon Bennett... yes! They could have ganged
up on him and hit him over the head with a
shovel." Genna chuckled.

"Genna, we must go up there and see what we
can find. I'll get crutches - you can drive me right
up to the door." Issy looked as though she was
about to leap up, plastered leg and all.

"Issy, hang on, before I go I must ask your advice
about something. You know more about medical
things than I do."

"Can't imagine what but fire away."

"It's my mother. She's not well and I don't know
what's the matter." Genna sighed. "She's gone so
thin lately, she looks really pale and says she's
dizzy. She was ready to pass out the other day."
Genna hesitated and then continued. "You know
the farm struggles to pay extra manpower. When it
came to Spring work one of Geoff Cordingly's lads
came to help, or I don't know how we would have
managed. Mum does too much now...as they both
get older they won't get any stronger. I cannot
leave them and can't see any future..." the tumble
of words broke off as Genna rubbed her fingers

across her forehead in an anxious gesture.

"Oh, Genna! I had no idea it was that bad."

"I know I'm capable of earning real money if only I had the chance. There's no answer to it for them or me. All there seems to be is overwork and debt for us. Oh, Issy, I didn't mean to dump all this on you. I'm so sorry."

"Considering you hauled me out of the bowels of the earth to save me from a horrible death the other day, I do consider I owe you one." Issy, if nothing else, was fair minded. "The immediate priority is you mother's health. You are imagining the worst, some sort of malignant disease?"

"I'm so worried about her."

"There could be simple answers - anaemia for instance. Suggest she comes down to the surgery and has a talk with father or William. A blood test wouldn't take a minute."

"That's just the problem, she won't agree. She's very reluctant to share anything about her physical self with doctors."

"I could talk to Wills, he's sure to come up with something even if it's only that saying... 'Change things where you can. Don't waste time worrying when you can't and heaven help you if you haven't the sense to see the difference'"

Genna smiled at Issy's misquote. "But that's the difficult bit, knowing the difference . Then her eyes widened as though a light bulb had been switched on in her head. "ISSY, YOU ARE SO RIGHT! I am worrying myself daft about mother and not doing a damn thing when maybe I could change things... do something positive to get her right. You may have just hit on the answer to my whole life in fact!"

It was Issy's turn to laugh. "Great! Just you nail Geoff Cordingly and see what he's remembered about 'The Croft'. All we can do then is find the mystery lover in the Gatenby family and we'll be on a roll."

At least, Genna acknowledged as she left, she seemed to have cheered up Issy and hopefully found some direction for her own endeavours.

CHAPTER ELEVEN

The day after Genna had visited Issy she made her way back to 'The Unicorn' car park. The truck had been left there while she did her afternoon run in the school minibus to pick up the children from Kettlington. She failed to notice the bearded face of Pete Murgatroyd looking out of the small back window at the rear of the pub. He watched her as she walked across the car park to the old truck and climbed in.

He scratched his head thoughtfully and ran his hand around the back of his neck in a gesture of frustration as she turned the truck and headed away from the pub quite unaware of her hidden observer.

It felt much warmer as Genna drove back to the farm and she smiled to herself as she noticed the lambs skipping and chasing across the field in the business of organised races as though they were training especially. It was important to succeed with the timing of their arrival. Frost or snow were bad enough but heavy rain in their first few weeks could mean losses too. Genna knew only too well the pitfalls of getting it wrong: jam or no jam and not much else on the table. Now these frisky little beings were no longer woolly scraps on four wobbly legs, they were finding more strength each day as the sun became warmer.

She must be optimistic, things really could become a lot better this summer, even new knickers. She must do as Issy said and not to worry when it could not change anything. She must choose the right moment and do something.

She turned off the road down the track to the farm. The way was heavily rutted and the truck bounced precariously making the vehicle rattle and squeak. She slowed down, fearful that something may drop off.

It was some minutes later when she arrived in the farmyard and from the passenger street she picked up her shopping and headed through the yard door into the kitchen to find her mother. "Mum… Mother, WHERE ARE YOU?" There was an appetising smell of cake from the oven but no sign of her mother. A small tabby cat came to rubber against her ankles meowing loudly. Genna bent down to stroke it after putting the shopping down on the scrubbed kitchen table. "Where's she gone, Cleo, do you know?"

She turned into the stone flagged passage to the back door of the farm which led out into the garden. She opened it to be greeted once again, this time by Fly, one of her father's border collies who worked with the sheep. The animal was slim and evenly marked in black and white with kind eyes and a silky feathery coat. He came up to Genna with an eager whine then set off towards the vegetable garden which stretched out behind a hedge to the palings and a broad oak tree bordering the slopes of the fields beyond.

The dog stopped and turned to look at Genna.

He could not have said 'come on' more clearly if he had spoken. Genna frowned and followed the animal.

She looked over the hedge and was greeted by a strange sight. Her mother was on her knees as though fighting to get up. She staggered in a helpless fashion almost achieving her aim to stand upright but she was no sooner on her feet that she toppled over like a drunk unable to find his balance. The neat rows of vegetables seem to enfold her. As Genna ran towards her she could see blood streaming down the side of her mother's face.

"Mum!" Genna knelt down beside her. "What's happened?"

The limp body lying in the soil groaned quietly in reply as the girl tried to lift her gently to a sitting position, at the same time rummaging in the pocket of her denim skirt for something to wipe the blood streaming from her mother's head.

Mrs. McFaiden, like Genna, had a mass of dark hair but with an almost Italian look about her colouring. The creamy skin, which at that moment had a greenish tinge to its paleness, was in sheer contrast to the dark redness of the blood trickling down the side of her face. As Genna attempted to lift her she realised just how light she was and felt the same stab of fear she had experience previously about the state of her mother's health.

"Genna! Oh, Genna! I went so swimmy...I quite lost my balance for a moment." She put her hand to the ground and eased herself against Genna's supporting arm. "Did I bang my head?" She put her fingers to her forehead to feel where Genna was mopping with her other hand to prevent blood trickling down her mother's neck. Jose MacFaiden gave her daughter an anxious look.

"Don't worry, Mum, heads always bleed like taps. I've learned that from kids, It's usually not half as bad as it looks. Put your arm around my shoulders and let's try to get you into the kitchen, then I can ring the doctor. That's it, hang on."

"No... no, Genna, don't be silly, there's no need for the doctor. I'm perfectly alright"

Genna was silent as she helped her mother to the door and down the passage.

Having reached the kitchen door without mishap she sat her down at one end of the old sofa which stood against the far kitchen wall, then lifted her legs onto the length of the cushions. "Now, tell me exactly what happened while I put on the kettle."

"Nothing much really, I'd just done a bit of digging, raked and weeded the plants...er, then I had one of my light headed turns. It's nothing unusual. I hadn't had much lunch - probably that. I found myself on the ground."

"You cannot go on like this, mother... I'm going to call the doctor."

"NO, Genna, I've told you I do not need the doctor." Her voice sounded sharp at having to tell her daughter something twice and Genna noted, quite unlike her usual self.

For a moment the girl hesitated, used to taking notice of her parents. She was tempted to shrug and let it go but some other idea inside her head took over. This could be the moment to change things for the better. "Mother, I've had enough of worrying about you and doing nothing. It may be something quite simple to put right." She turned to look at her mother's bad colour and thought of Issy's advise about a blood test taking only two minutes to see if she was anaemic.

"Genna..." she started, then gave a weak unhappy shrug of acceptance quite to the girls amazement that it had been so easy. She quickly looked up the number to telephone the surgery.

Harvey, his partner and William were all out, the receptionist told her, but if it was urgent she would pass on the message and one of them could call. Genna replied that it was.

The kettle boiled with a noisy whistle and the tea was soon brewed. Genna took the cake out of the oven; it was rather crisp and although it was still warm she insisted her mother ate a slice with her tea. The colour seemed to return to her cheeks and she looked quite her old self.

"Look, Genna, ring the surgery back and tell them I don't need a visit. I feel just fine now; the tea did the trick. You can't waste their time like this. Go on, do it now."

"Mother!" Genna was ready for a fight but there was no need for it, at that moment there was a knock on the door and in walked William, medical bag in hand. "Hello, Genna, I understand you called the surgery. How can I help?"

"William! The patient's right here," she held out a hand towards the couch. "This is my mother."

"Ah… Mrs. McFaiden." William's slow smile, as Genna had noticed before, gave a warmth that encouraged confidence as he shook Jose's hand.

"Dr Farrington, we haven't met but I did meet your father some years ago."

"Tell me about the problem, how did you cut your head?"

"Oh, I'm alright, it's a fuss about nothing. I just went a bit dizzy and lost my balance. Would you like a cup of tea?"

"Mother, William needs the proper facts. I found her twenty minutes ago stretched out on the vegetable plot. She looked far worse that she does now. She's lost a bit of weight recently and it's not the first time she's felt faint and dizzy."

William looked across to Jose who said nothing but did not deny any of it. He declined the tea and went on to take Jose's pulse and blood pressure. As he was doing this he asked questions in his quiet easy manner. The questions went on for quite some time and Genna congratulated herself that something must come out of this to help her mother.

"May I ask you, Mrs. MacFaiden, what sort of health did your parents have?" He was carefully cleaning the cut with gentle hands.

Genna tensed. Her mother was very touchy on

the subject of her ancestry. She had been brought up by an older couple in Kettlington who had died before Genna was born, but some how she always seemed reluctant to offer information about her origins. Genna knew from small comments she had made her mother had not been mistreated, on the contrary the couple had been very kind. She waited curiously for her reply.

"I cannot see how that…"she began and then stopped. William waited. "The people who brought me up were not my natural parents. I never knew who they were. I understand I was adopted."

"Oh, I see. Right." William nodded.

The tension Genna had experience for a moment and even dreaded, disappeared as if by magic and she cast her mind back as to why she felt anxious. She recalled she had never actually heard her mother say she was adopted. She wondered now at the truth of it. She knew there was another factor, her mother reacted strangely to gypsies. She was scared of them quite irrationally and would go nowhere near if they were about. Could there be a connection?

Genna remembered when two Romany caravans had appeared down the lane not far from the farm track and her mother had insisted her father check they were not coming nearer the farm. A day or so later visitors had appeared, a woman with a small child dressed in colourful Romany get up stood at the farm door. Two pairs of dark eyes peered keenly from beneath tangles of wavy dark hair. The woman offered to tell fortunes and the child carried a basked with assorted, simple, handmade articles and charms. Genna had answered their knock and gone to fetch her mother.

"Get rid of them quickly... There are some eggs on the table - give them some and tell them to be careful as they go because the dogs are vicious and bite strangers."

"But, Mum, the dogs have never..."

"We do not want them back, Genna, now go on, tell them"

Genna had noticed her mother was trembling. She had never seen her act like that before; she was not an unkind or bigoted woman and not usually scared of much either.

Later she had questioned her father about her mother's odd attitude to gypsies. He had smiled quietly. Half asleep in the chair.

"Aye, she won't have any gypos about the place. She thinks they're after her."

"But, Dad why should she think that?"

"Something in her childhood? Try asking her. You may learn more than I ever have." He was off to sleep again hardly before finishing the sentence.

Genna stood there remembering as she listening to William questions and sensing the professionalism and directness, the search for information to tie things in that mattered. As he attended to the cut on her mother's head, Genna suddenly realised the obvious connection between her mother's origins and gypsies. She looked at her mother's dark wavy hair and her creamy complexion. Had Jose's real parents been gypsies and had she been afraid they may come back for her? She broke off the chain of thought as William moved towards the table and his bag.

"Well, Mrs. McFaiden, I think all your problems - loss of weight, tiredness and dizziness, may be related to a touch of sugar imbalance, in medical terms, a late onset diabetes. This may well be corrected by attention to diet and eating at the right times. I'm telling you this based on the preliminary tests I've done and you won't be anxious waiting. I would like you to come to the surgery in the morning so we can assess the situation more accurately. But I see no cause for you to worry - this can be put to rights quite simply. In the meantime this is what I would like you to do." William picked up his note pad and wrote simple instructions for his patient to follow.

Genna looked across at him, she could easily have flung her arms around his neck and hugged him in gratitude. If her mother's problems could be pinpointed so easily and maybe rectified by diet alone, her fears about her health must be far less threatening than she had imagined. She felt tears prickling her eye, she blinked quickly but was aware they had not escaped William's notice. His diagnosis made her realise just how worried she had been. She must tell Issy what a relief her advise had proved to be.

"Just come to the surgery tomorrow morning and

see our practice nurse first, then see me and we'll have this sorted in no time."

"Thank you, Dr. Farrington, I'll be there tomorrow."

Genna walked William to the yard door and followed him out in the late afternoon sunshine as he walked towards his car. "Thanks for coming so quickly, William, I have been hoping I could coax her into coming to see you before this."

"It was simple, I happened to be quite near on a call when the surgery caught me on my mobile." He stopped as they drew level with his estate car and he turned to look at her . "You were really anxious about her, weren't you?"

"Yes."

"In fact even thought it was something far worse?"

"I thought she must be really ill, she has lost so much weight."

"Genna is there somewhere we could talk for a minute?"

Genna led him to the orchard with its daffodils. They sat on the bench and for a moment the grandeur of the view over the valley grabbed their attention. The early evening light was golden, filtering dreamily through the small trees. Apart from a lamb who, having mislaid its mother and was telling the whole world in plaintive high bleats, the peacefulness was compelling, outdone only by the vastness of the land sweeping down away from them.

"This is really worth having," William broke the silence,

"It's one of the things that keeps me here."

"And the others?"

"Mother and Father and what they value and would hate to lose."

William nodded his understanding before he replied. "Genna, you could have talked to me about your mother. I would have been only too willing to listen. Together we could have thought of a way to persuade her to visit the surgery."

"She resisted it quite stubbornly, she even tried to put me off calling you today and it hardly seemed fair to ask you in the pub. In fact it was something Issy said earlier that may me decide to go against her."

"I'm very glad you did. Diabetes is a very treatable condition especially as it does not appear to be severe, but I'll soon know everything with the tests. I suppose I wondered if you found me unapproachable." Williams grey eyes were discerning as always as he asked.

"Good heavens, no, William, and I just cannot tell you how grateful I am we have got to the bottom of it."

"Good, because I feel you an I have...we seem to understand each other." He looked at her with an expression that made her want to reach out and touch his face, tell him she felt it too... oh how much she felt it.

"I know farming is not easy these days." William

turned away to the landscape."

"No, but it is worth it, if like dad, that's all you want to do. He eats sleeps and breathes all this." She spread out her hands at the great dimensions of the land before them.

"Is he buoyant about it all?"

"He does sometimes go a bit quiet , not really depressed but...why? No, don't tell me, I read the papers and see the news, you're thinking of the suicide figures they've published lately? Farmers have the worst and rising." Genna lifted her head to the heavens and breathed a deep breath.

"Genna, no..." William slipped an arm around her shoulders and Genna resisted the urge to rest her head against him. "I didn't mean to shove that in your face. The figures are not a lot different from those for GPs especially in the last few years with the changes in practice workings. It's just sensible to keep a check and know he's OK. If I remember your father he's a fighter, just quiet with it."

"That's him, for sure, not like that guy the other day further up the Dale?"

"Abbot's farm?" No, the odds were stacked against him. Father was called out to pick up the bits. Are they selling up?"

"Yes, his health was poor, but he had two sons, that's the awful thing. They can't have given him the right support."

"With somebody like you for a daughter, Eddy can't go far wrong!" William smiled his slow, easy, smile then bent his head towards her as he squeezed her shoulders and kissed her cheek affectionately in passing. "Going down that shaft the other day to rescue my sister took guts. Both John and I were full of admiration."

Genna felt her face flame and was quite unaware how attractive she looked, her white T shirt crisp and clean against the denim, her dark hair tumbling round her neck. The curly lashed blue eyes regarding him steadily. She had to clench her knuckles tightly to stop herself returning his affectionate gesture in double rations. Instead she stood up and assumed a businesslike manner. " I expect you've got loads to do and I'm holding you up. And oh, by the way I forgot to congratulate you on your engagement to Debora. I hope you'll be very happy." She stuck out a formal hand and William shook it. She was almost defiant - a don't mess with me air about her.

William gave her a wry look. "Thanks, the lovely Debora, I can't do right for doing wrong at the moment...but yes...I must get going. Don't forget, anything you want to know about your mother's condition or problems, I'm here." So saying he turned towards the gate and she was left looking out over the daffodils, the valley and the emptiness of the landscape.

It was later lying in bed, staring into the dark, the thought came to Genna that although she had done something quite definite about her mother, her plan of action concerning William had no form or shape. Should there be a plan of action? There were , she decided, three options, firstly she could go on dreaming about him, biting her lip in frustration like today, secondly, she could put a stop to the whole thing, push him out of her thoughts, or thirdly, she could go for it, do what Issy would do and make it quite clear what she wanted, after all he wasn't married yet! She wouldn't dare... would she? She shivered at the thought. Maybe the real question was, could she stand looking a complete fool if it did not come off?

Diary Notes.
SUMMER 1942

The war drags on and in North Africa things are awful. We have withdrawn from Libya and the British forces have surrendered at Tobruk. Nobody is very happy except me!

The most amazing thing has happened. Since the Spring I have had to drive different officers at times but my Romeo boss lent me the other day to a pilot officer who had to get to London in a hurry; some sort of emergency in his family. My boss told him, and he knew I was able to hear, that I was the best woman driver he had ever come across and he would stake his life with me, (more likely his reputation which I hold in the palm of my hand; how cynical I am these days.)

As it turned out this particular pilot officer really did have his life to thank me for. His name is

George Bigham-Wade but he gets Gee for short.

My orders were to wait for him and bring him back to base. We had to set off very early and it turned out to be quite a trip.

The drive to the city was uneventful and we made spasmodic polite conversation. I had to keep my eyes on the road when I was dying to look at the buildings half blown away by bombs, windows with no glass only curtains blowing in the breeze. I waited quite some time while he attended to his business. It was still light when I drove back and not so far from home there was a terrifying incident. A Messerschmitt 109 and a Spitfire came ripping over us out of the blue at house height in a 'dog fight' obviously hell bent on destruction.

The peace was shattered as these two climbed up to gain some height and have another go at one another. We could see them quite clearly as we came to the top of a small rise, the countryside spread out before us. Suddenly they were coming our way and we knew if they came low we could be in a dangerous spot for stray bullets.

I was trying to decide where to pull of the road and take cover when a motorbike despatch rider appeared coming the other way. He turned to look at the 'dog fight' and I realised he had not seen us. It all happened very quickly and I managed to avoid a head on crash by taking very definite evasive action and putting the car in the nearest ditch!

We missed the man by the smallest of margins; I could feel his helmet whizzing past the windscreen.

(I'd become pretty good at missing pedestrians!)

The impact threw us all over the place and when we managed to slowly unravel ourselves we were up to our eyes in grass and mud as we climbed on hands and knees out of the car. My first reaction was that my skirt had split on the door and I was aware my passenger was looking at my stocking tops, as he was there beside me.

As well as being scratched and bruised I was filled with confusion because he would undoubtedly have expected to see issue bloomers (passion killers) which he didn't. These are so hot in summer and I had on my one pair of lacy French knickers. He could not drag his eyes away. God knows what else he saw! I could hear mother say 'I hope you kept your knees together' I don't believe I did! The girls have commented on the fact that my thighs are blessedly slim and some how this made me feel really wicked...I enjoyed it! He was so nice.

I found a safety pin for my skirt and with me trying to look composed, we managed to get onto the road again after a combined effort with the despatch rider to push the car out of the ditch. Mechanically it was in one piece and the engine ticket over with only a few splutters as we set off. The 'dog fight' had been forgotten.

After we arrived back my passenger insisted we have a drink once I'd changed. Wearing civvies nobody bothers much about officers fraternizing with the ranks unless bad luck produces some wretched striped WAAF who spots a familiar face.

My man was quiet and charming, not a bit like a lot of the pilot officers who, by nature of their job, can be a wild, noisy lot sometimes,. Who can blame them when for so many of them tomorrow never comes?

We sat in a quiet corner of the pub and I was terribly shy at first but eventually we talked because we found we had so much in common. We had both spent our lives with our noses in books instead of experiencing much of real life. For him too, the war had altered that.

Now we are friends and I seem to be going around with a permanent smile on my face, at the same time secretly praying every night that nothing terrible happens to him.

CHAPTER TWELVE

As well as wondering what to do about William, Genna's mind harked back to the conversation with Issy about Emily Gatenby. She saw her in her mind's eye, not really the woman with a secret but the young girl the same age as herself.

As she carried out small mundane tasks like hanging clothes away on her rail in the bedroom or cleaning her teeth, Genna began to see a picture of the person old Mrs. Clarke had told her about, quiet, rather serious and yet riding horses with confident expertise and driving a car like a lunatic. What had happened in her life, what sort of things had really motivated her and how had they led to the body buried in the woods? The picture expanded from an unlikely source.

Issy had phoned and asked Genna if she could get away to meet her in the village. Issy said she would have to get out of the house or she may explode with the hellish boredom of her own company, right before her moter's watchful eye. Her mother was taking scones for a Bring and Buy sale at ten o' clock. She would somehow negotiate the back seat of Marjorie Farrington's small car which would accommodate her plastered leg. Genna found her at ten thirty in Bessie's tea shop, leg stretched out.

"I never imagined it would be a big deal to drive into Elvingdale with my mother. Just goes to show what a bit of deprivation will do for you." She Grinned at Genna. "How's you Mum? William said he's seen her but not why or how. Very discreet our Wills."

Genna told her the story of the visit and its outcome. "You did a good job there Isso. I think we're about level in the good turns department. She just has to stick to the regime they prescribed and she should be OK.

"Great. You know finding that body at 'The Croft' has made this place more of a focal point round here than ever. When we drove into the village it was beginning to fill up with visitors. I don't want to complain but I wish there were fewer of them, we only just found a parking place."

"Don't let Bessie hear you say that," Genna replied. "Anyway I thought we were supposed to be politically correct and share the countryside with others."

"Not in my back yard!"

"What's not in your back yard?" Bessie was next to them looking quizzically at Issy.

"Oh, Bessie, we were talking about the body up at 'The Croft'. Did you ever have anything to do with Emily Gatenby?" Issy was deft at distracting tactics.

"Only one thing I ever heard was that she went into the WAAF in the war, so somebody once said... and her mother was furious. She wanted her to stay at home. But y'know how it is here, gossip drifts about the place. What can I get you, Genna, coffee?"

"The WAAF!" Issy rolled big eyes after Bessie had

departed. "Listen, Gen, I cannot wait. Let's go up to 'The Croft' this afternoon. Have you got time?"

Issy was on a roll again, Genna noted but ...maybe she was right, Issy's steamroller stuff could work. "I told Pete I may not be here at lunch time and he said it would be okay, he could manage, so I am free until it's time to do the school run." Genna notice Issy hesitate. Was she aware, Genna wondered, that it would mean less wage for her at the end of the week?

"Look, Gen, if you..." but she stopped and tailed off with another thought. "Have you brought the key?"

"Yes, it's in my purse."

"I have to pop into see John about something but you could come too, then take me up in the racing truck and we'll go for it."

Genna smiled, Issy's enthusiasm was catching.

"Right, you've talked me round."

The blonde apparition with the blue mascara told Issy in no uncertain terms that Mr. Glendenning was out and would not be back that afternoon. Leonie, however, did not stop there. "You don't mind me asking but would you be the Miss Farrington who had the awful fall last Sunday?" the Scottish burr enquired.

"Don't mind and yes, that's me."

"You were out walking with Mr. Glendenning, weren't you?"

Genna waited, looking vaguely at the property

boards full of country cottages, but aware at the same time, of a certain tension in the air. Leonie's question sounded almost scolding.

Issy nodded "You don't miss much do you?"

"Weell, perhaps I shouldn't say this but it may do you a favour. It's just that between you an me... you have to watch him." The blonde head leaned forward conspiratorially and Genna could only just catch the words.

"He's an awful flirt." Leonie smoothed a navy nailed hand round her hair pausing for effect and hardly hiding her smugness. "It was not long ago he got caught with a married lady in Kettlington with his trousers down... by her husband. "Did you know that?" The whispered Scots tones were hard to catch but Genna managed.

Issy did not miss a beat as she looked Leonie straight in the eyes. "Yes, I'm not really surprised. You heard I fell down a mine shaft when it happened?" It was Issy's turn for conspiracy.

Leonie nodded eagerly, ears almost visibly rabbit sized to catch what Issy had to say next.

"Well, don't tell a soul." Issy bent closer towards the girls expectant face, "but we were dancing round that shaft stark naked with grouse feathers in our hair when it happened and I fell." She tapped her leg and nodded. "I have to admit I don't regret a thing, it was a REAL turn on. Bye" She pivoted on her heel awkwardly, leaning on her stick and opened the shop door for Genna, who by this time was struggling not to explode with mirth, not entirely at Issy's statement but Leonie's face and its astounded expression.

The two girls made their way into the street, Issy hanging onto Genna's arm and grinding her teeth with rage and suppressed emotion.

"It's got to be true, hasn't it? The little cow!"

"Issy, he was sure to have baggage - a past, he's too good looking not to. Doesn't necessarily mean he's bad. Seems a nice guy to me."

"OH, Genna! Do you really think so? I'm so daft about him?" Issy wailed.

"Mmm, know what you mean." And she did, only too well. The ache for William had become worse and she found herself constantly lying in bed at night thinking about him, his easy smile as he had kissed her cheek when they had sat in the orchard. But still she had made no decision about him.

"Look, Issy, you wait here and I'll drive the truck down from the pub. You're not supposed to walk much on that leg."

Issy gave a long sigh at the fraughtness of it all and nodded.

DIARY NOTES.
AUTUMN 1942.

I have been out with Gee quite a few times now. I don't know how long my happiness will last. Gee is marvellous, so exciting and yet a kind man. My opinion seems to matter to him, although he is more worldly than I. His life is all risk and danger being a bomber pilot. Search lights everywhere and flak pours around them. Each night he is on flights is a nightmare that he may not come back. He doesn't talk much about it. I don't talk about him to the girls but I learn plenty about what goes on as I listen quietly to them.

When we are together Gee and I, it is as though the flood gates of a lifetime have been opened. I am going to make the most of it while I can. Please God don't let him be killed.

If only we knew how long the war could go on. Churchill is an incredible leader and there's hope now that we will after all, pull through. The country may be flattened to its roots by this awful barrage from the skies but we still seem to live to fight another day.

I have discovered that Gee is very well connected. His father is Sir Anthony Bigham-Wade. They have a very grand place in the country but part of it has been taken over by the army. His family are living in their London residence at the moment and they are, like royalty, determined to stay there despite the bombing. Anyway his father has a high up job in the Ministry, whatever that means. Oh, my darling Gee, I wonder what will become of us.

'The Croft' looked much the same as it had done before, Genna notes as she pointed out the space where the window of the Rose room could just be seen amongst the thick creeper. "Look, Issy, in the middle hidden under those leaves."

"Yes, I can just see a window. What a shame the poor old place has been let go so badly."

"Well, it's the garden mostly, inside the house is pretty solid. Come on, hold my arm and I'll show you.

Getting Issy in and out of the truck had been a conquest of determination over impossibility but determination was not in short supply with Issy and it was not long before Genna was helping her round to the back of the house with its decrepit porch.

"This is weird." Issy shivered as they entered the kitchen. If I came here by myself I'd be scared to death."

"I didn't have time to be at first. I was so amazed when the key fitted I just walked straight in. It was upstairs...the bed sock..." She gave a sharp intake of breath, shutting out the vision that was trying to creep in.

"I haven't really seen it yet - the key." Isss held out her hand to take it from Genna. "I see what you mean about the open metal work, it's the shape of a Tudor rose. So do we find a suitable rose and hope it covers a key hole?"

"It's only a guess. I haven't tried it yet." Genna ran her fingers along a dusty ledge, giving Issy time to rest her leg before going up the stairs. "You okay now?"

"Sure, let's get going."

The stairs nevertheless were no easy matter and Issy had to do a sort of crablike sideways ascent.

"Don't worry. I'm right behind you," Genna told her.

"Oh, I know, if anything jumps out it will get me first." Issy giggled nervously

"Course, I'm not stupid."

The stairs creaked ominously as they climbed. They turned a corner and Issy slowed up, the pot taking its toll. Genna overtook her peering cautiously up towards the stair head as though she expected some grotesque image to materialise from the dusty, dim corridor.

"As far as I can make out it should be in the longer gap between these two doors." Genna pointed to the bedroom doors. "So the idea is to feel the Tudor roses and find one that isn't solid to the panelling or maybe moves. You start there and I'll go further along."

The silence that followed was eerie, magnifying small noises made by the wind in another part of the house. "Tell you what, I wouldn't stay here two minutes on my own." Issy muttered as they searched. "I could swear there was somebody downstairs."

"Issy, for heavens sake, we'll never get this done if you go on. We'll be fleeing out of here scared to death like I did the first time."

The search progressed along the wall as the two looked for a thin gap in the panelling that could indicate a door, at the same time feeling the small carved flowers in the corners of the design to see if they moved.

"GENNA!... I'VE GOT IT!" It was a shout and Genna jumped visibly

"Issy, ... Good grief! I thought it was Emily Gatenby back from the dead. You scared the wits out of me. Is there a key hole or...?"

"No, there's no key hole but it doesn't seem as solid as the rest. I can't push the rose out of the way, or anything. If I had some leverage on it I think it may turn...AND LOOK, there's a tiny space between the edges of the panelling here."

Genna ran her fingers over the rose and felt it move slightly. ""Let's have another look at the key." Genna fumbled in her haste to get it out of her pocket then, as it lay across the palm of here hand the two inspected it. Carefully Genna matched the open rose head to the curve of the flower. It clicked over snugly. The two exchanged wide eyed looks. Genna gave the key a wiggle like using a spanner round a nut. Effortlessly the door that fitted so neatly into the panelling swung open inwardly like an ordinary door but making the girls gasp as a dimly furnished room appeared before them.

CHAPTER THIRTEEN

For a moment the surprise of actually finding the Rose room left both the girls shocked and they stood taking in the details of the space before them. The light, from what they now recognised as the Tudor rose shaped window, was almost obliterated. It could never have been a very well lit room but the creeper and the grime on the glass itself obstructed their vision.

They stepped forward cautiously as though something might be lurking there but in doing so Genna knew they were not stepping forward, they were going back in time. The room was from the past. She looked at Issy with incredulous eyes.

They could make out a tall mahogany mantelpiece with a top shelf and lower shelf, the ends of which were held apart by beautifully carved struts. An outdated gas fire had been fitted into the grate and was surrounded by what must have once been gleaming ornate victorian tiles.

A gate-legged table with candy twist legs placed near the window had the chair beside it pushed to one side as though someone had just got up and left the room. In an alcove opposite the fireplace there was a day bed with an elegant rolled over end, the satin striped cover dingy with dust. The colours of the Indian carpet on the floor were hardly discernable and a stray rod of sunshine picked out the disturbed motes of dust rising in the air.

Issy broke the silence, "Just LOOK at this." Issy was pointing to the ceiling where, from the middle of a circle of ornate plastering, a light fitting hung on chains. Multicoloured sections of glass, leaded apart gave it a Tiffany image. "What d'you think? Suspended money if you ask me?"

"Whoever cleared the house must have missed all this, even if it had been in the deeds," Genna murmured. "The police must have missed it too but of course if they didn't know it existed it's hardly surprising."

The girls gazed around them taking in the room from the centre of its floor. "There's a gas ring on a tray with room for a kettle, you can see a watermark."

Issy pointed. "It gives you the feeling somebody spent a lot of time in here. Look at the radio." Genna noted old fashioned church window wireless set on a small table.

"It's really like a bedsit." Issy knew about bedsits.

"What about this bookcase?" Genna's delight was obvious at the sight of the large array of books behind glass doors. "Look 'King Solomon's Mines' and 'She', The Thiry-nine Step,' such treasures, would you believe?"

"Does all this hark back to the harbouring a spy theory?"

"How on earth are we to know, but look at the day bed; you could sleep on that. There's something quite Victorian about it... and yet a touch of how I imagine the forties to be. Let's see if we can coax a bit more light in. Maybe the window will open."

Issy limped across the room and pushed heavy dark curtains out of the way releasing more dust while Genna attempted to find out how the window opened.

"There's a catch and it looks as though it should tilt." She managed to release the catch with difficulty and then pushed hard at the window. At first it resisted all her strength, then Issy lent a hand and it gave way in a rush nearly sending the pair sprawling onto the floor. Issy grabbed at a chair to save herself as light and air flooded into the room. The two laughed nervously at the release of tension.

Genna dusted herself down and looked around once more. "Issy have you seen that lovely little cupboard in the middle of the mantelpiece. It's so nicely carved between the two levels and the mahogany or whatever is still shiny?

Issy limped over and pulled on the dewdrop fastening on the small door. "Locked of course."

"There's probably a key somewhere; look in the ornaments; people always stuff keys in the nearest thing they can find."

At that precise moment something happened which made the two girls freeze. In itself common place but in their situation potential for calamity, the sound of a car, easily spotted through the open window, came closer as it crunching on the gravel. Genna flew over to look as Issy limped towards the door ready to leave.

"It's the police, coming through the gate. I'm going to shut the window slowly and hope they don't see."

"Damn it, we'll have to go outside and brave it out, or they're sure to come and look now they've seen the truck." Issy glanced across at Genna desperately. "We cannot shut ourselves in here, we don't know how to get out, there are no roses inside. Anyway we don't want them to know about this."

Genna nodded her head, agreeing to the conspiracy without realising it while in the process of closing the window. It sounded like sense. The window clicked into place and she quickly followed Issy through the panelling door, pulling it closed behind her.

Issy was ahead hopping and clattering down the stairs, doing her best not to fall. "If we can just get out off the back door we can tell them... anything but what on earth have they come for?"

"Still keeping an eye on the grave site, I imagine. Genna heard a car door shut as they reached the bottom of the stairs and skidded round the corner to the kitchen.

"What are we going to say?" Genna gasped with the effort of helping Issy and beginning to wonder if it had been sense to make a dash for it.

"Don't know yet...I'm thinking..

"What about losing the dog and we've been searching?"

Through the kitchen and out of the back door, Genna stuffed her hand into her pocket for the key. It wasn't there. Had she left it in the Rose room? Panic threatened but feeling in her other pocket relief shot through her as her fingers touched the metal.

The pair were walking nonchalantly away from the other side of the porch door as two uniformed police came round the corner.

"Ah, just the sort of help we need. Am I pleased to see you? We've lost my dog, she's a Boxer. I don't suppose you've seen her roaming around? Issy was the coolest being on the planet and Genna suddenly felt like a schoolgirl about to giggle.

She sucked in a quiet deep breath still catching up from the escape. She tried to look concerned about the dog as Issy proclaimed a highly believable tale of woe as to who they were and how long they'd been looking for Fifi.

"Are you still working here? If you get fed up, come on down to 'the Rectory' and have a cup of tea," confidence was everything Genna noted.

"We were about to take down some of the yellow tape. We just came round here to see who the truck belonged to. We'll keep a look out for your dog, Miss Farrington. Sorry we can't stop for tea. Hope you find her, Bitches don't usually wander far though, do they?" The older man called over his shoulder as he turned to go.

Issy hobbled over to the stable block calling Fifi loudly until the police disappeared. Looking to see if they were out earshot, she limped back and the two collapsed over one another gasping and sighing in relief.

"ISSY! He did not believe a word of that. He must have twigged we were nosying."

"I don't care, we haven't done any harm and what a FIND! We HAVE to go back now and start digging around properly."

"Not right now, I don't have time but yes, we have to go back soon."

"It's all going to fit now, after we've been and really sussed the place, we can say we found the key looking for Fifi and then we can…"

But Genna wasn't listening. "It was all such a strange time warp," she murmured.

DIARY NOTES
November 1942

The battle for El Alamein is at last over with a victory for the Eighth Army and General Montgomery. Everyone believes this is the 'turn of the tide' in the war. We are going to be victorious and send the Hun packing. Fear has taken a step away from us but things are by no means assured.

I have never been as close to anyone in my whole life as I am to Gee. Can it be possible that war should be a happy time? The fear that I could lose him on any moonlit night is never far away and makes the whole affaire somehow more desperate because he and I are lovers.

With Gee showing me the way I have taken that great step. The first time was in an old hay loft, with straw in the most peculiar places. We even laughed when we made love and it was better than I ever imagined it could be.

When one considers the mechanics of the thing, it sounds so odd but in reality at its heights, it is a flight of the emotions to a sun filled heaven. Now I know what life is all about and why some people have special smiles on their faces, I am one of them.

Gee is very careful not to hurt me, or get me into trouble. I think he knows a lot more about it than I do... I have not asked but I really don't care. I would do anything for him. I cannot believe it is me. I have told nobody about my relationship with him except mother and I have written to her with all the 'right' information. The rest I am hugging to myself because if anything happens to him or if it goes wrong, I think I could face it better if nobody knew.

The following few days saw a breakdown in the weather with rain and wind tearing at the new found lacy green of the trees. Genna was busy helping her father and Issy had no means of getting up to 'The Croft' on her own.

The ensuing telephone conversations between the two girls covered the merits of withholding information from the Police - were they, or weren't they and did it matter anyway? They would ultimately inform the authorities when they had

investigated the Rose room fully and simply say
they had found the key while looking for Issy's dog
and only just discovered how the mechanism
worked.

"There is an important eleventh commandment,"
Issy stated.

"Thou shalt not be caught at it!"

"Yes, as I told John when we talked about his faux
pas with that married bird in Kettlington."

"You asked him about it?" Genna sounded
astonished.

"I explained how, in revenge, I told Leonie we
danced around the mine shaft starkers, grouse
feathers and all that."

Issy's recklessness never failed to amaze Genna."
What one earth did he say?"

"He fell about laughing and said it served her
right for splitting. She's barking anyway."

"So it is true about the woman?"

"Yes, but it was a couple of years ago in his mad
youth and he was very sorry for the wife who had a
sod of a husband."

Genna noted John had talked himself nicely out
of that one.

"So that's the end of Leonie?"

"I certainly hope so. Anyway we're in the pub
Monday."

"Great! Maybe we'll have the chance to discuss
another foray into the past." Genna hoped Issy
would not be tempted to tell William about the
Rose room. She died to ask about him but Issy had

intimated earlier that he had been moody and unhappy, all to do with Debora, she was sure.

Telling Issy how she felt about William was a tempting trap but Issy might easily drop a hint to her brother. Where Issy's mouth was concerned discretion was best.

CHAPTER FOURTEEN

Saturday was a day Genna would never forget
and for more than one reason. The first part of it
was better than expect.

The pub was going to be very busy from
lunchtime onwards, all to do with the PCRCC Club
This, in fact, was one of Pete's babies and it had a
name he had chosen - 'The Physically Challenged
Rock Climbers and Cavers' but the Pissy Arsies was
what it came out as, taking into account they all
drank like thirsty camels. The pub lunch was free to
this collection of past dare devils, or those whose
luck had simply run out and were now in
wheelchairs, sported elbow crutches, or harboured
some disability collected in their particular field of
conflict with nature.

The upside for Genna, was the fact that William,
now a member of the Fell Rescue, would be
talking, helping and taking a general interest in the
plights of the various members. The downside was
that she wouldn't get much time to speak to him.

When she had first spotted him coming over to
the bar her heart had done its usual somersault.
She had made a special effort to look good
knowing he would be there. Her dark hair shone
and her skin glowed from being outside a lot of the
time. The blue/grey top was the most flattering
thing she possessed and it did a good job making
her clear eyes look bluer than ever. The fresh
uncomplicated look she presented to the world

was offset by a hint that she was disciplined and knew what she was doing.

She watched the unmistakable blond head as William threaded his way between the tables, sticks and crutches. His navy T shirt showing of sturdy shoulders.

"Well, lack of mobility doesn't seem to have tamed this lot," he looked around at the boisterous company.

"Certainly not." Genna pulled a pint of the lager she knew he liked and attempted to look as though nothing in the world mattered. Her insides did the familiar tarantella which radiated to her hands and made them shake.

"How's your mother doing?"

"Just fine - seems pretty stable, thank goodness, rather thanks to a certain Dr. Farrington. She managed a small smile but even that made her lips quiver out of control. What an extraordinary thing love was that it could turn someone into this trembling jelly state, she reflected.

"I'm going to be around for some time, so just... er, whistle me up if you need any help or...anything." He spread his hands out while gazing at her, "standing there, you look good enough to eat and I wouldn't be surprised to find those here who may try." He raised an eyebrow, his grey eyes crinkling into a smile as he carried off the lager.

Genna would have like to have thrown her arms in the air and shouted at the sheer joyous delight of his compliment and she felt her face taking on a warm glow. It wasn't just his good looks - well maybe it was, it was more the magnetism of his personality. He was not the only one to see it, Issy had mentioned how Wills was a people magnet and how pleased her father had been at his increasing popularity in the practice. Not that it was doing Genna any good at all, but a girl could dream, couldn't she?

She looked up from her revelry straight into the eyes of Geoff Cordingly It made her jump and her hand flew to her mouth. "Geoff! I'm sorry, I was miles away."

"Aye...I could tell that." He commented dryly, shaking his head. "Pint of shandy when you've got a minute to spare."

"Genna grinned knowing his sarcasm was humorous rather than critical. "Geoff, I was wondering about you. Did you find the thing about 'The Croft' you'd forgotten?" To her surprise Geoff's face shut down making him look almost furtive.

"Aye, I did an' all," he looked from side to side as though in fear of being heard. "Not for general consumption though. Suppose I should 'a told bobbies but I don't fancy being called a loopy ol' milkman," he growled. "I'll tell y' about it some time when it's quiet." He gave her his money and turned away leaving Genna completely curious as to what he could possibly have remembered and what Issy would make of it."

Pete, to his credit, was making a good job of

looking after his guests. Drinks had to be paid for but food sold to the public in general went to charity, not a large sum but a nice little help towards equipment, or oddments needed which could not be met by the budget. He was also giving out large dollops of bonhomie, cajoling and laughing, making everyone feel wanted. Genna watched him; his beard and size stood out from the crowd and she thought what a basically decent guy he was in spite of his wandering eye.

It was when William came over to the bar for more drink that she plucked up courage to ask the question rattling around in her mind.

"No Deborah today?"

"She's on flights...Rome, I believe. It takes me all my time to remember which end of Europe she's going to next."

"It must be a really interesting job."

"It's people - same as this, " he turned towards the scene in the pub, " only a bit more varied. You could do it with your eyes closed."

At the time Genna dismissed the remark but when she thought about it in the rare quiet moment between pulling pints, she realised he was right, she would have easily been able to do the job. If only she was not tied to the farm. The old sense of frustration presented itself and she was left with the same hollow feeling of nowhere to go.

DIARY NOTES.
Spring 1943.

January the Luftwaffe began more terrible raids on London. We hear stories about people living in the underground stations, sleeping on the platforms, some because it is the safest place to shelter, others because they have no homes left. In some streets there are houses standing but they are not safe to occupy. The few possessions these poor souls have are beside them and they sing and share their food with a marvellous and determined spirit.

Gee has been moved further South and although I do not see him as much, we are still very close and he says he loves me more than ever.

He is likely to be involved with some top secret bombing mission over Germany. He can't tell me about it; all I now is they fly Lancasters and with his crew, make a very close team. It is top secret and he cannot reveal any more. From what he says it sounds horribly risky. He is so brave. I expect that is why he has been chosen, although I know he is often scared and does not want to die. Please, dear God, let him survive.

May, 1943: *It has happened as I dreaded it would. Gee's Lancaster was hit with flak on the way back from a massive raid over Germany. The mission was highly successful and did untold damage to the Germans. Why, oh why has it got to be so awful - people blown to bits, not just soldiers but mothers and children? I know they are Germans*

*but they are still human beings just as we are.
Although he did not tell me this himself, we heard
on the news of the success of the raid but there
were a great many Lancasters lost and the flak was
horrendously heavy. He came home on a wing and
a prayer, as they say. He was very lucky to survive.
He hit his head when they almost crash landed but
he got himself and the boys down on the ground in
once piece and he is alive!*

*Gee is in hospital and concussed although he
came round once. Over the next week he lapsed
into unconsciousness for two days. It has been hell
because I was not able to see him. He started to
come round for short spells after that and now he is
fully conscious, although he has other injuries and
burns on his arms.*

*The hospital is quite a way but I am managing to
wheedle visits with various excuses. There are
always ways when a car is available and being a
driver. I have to tell all sorts of outrageous lies,
what's more, I do it with conviction.*

It was past three o'clock before the PCRCC
members began to disband, being helped to
wheelchairs abandoned outside, along with cars,
lifts or whichever way they had arrived. Pete was
fully occupied and William had left to drive
someone home.

Genna was about to go back to the farm and help
with work there before she returned to the pub for
the evening, when Geoff Cordingly beckoned her

over to a corner seat. There were a few stragglers around the pub but not within earshot of his corner. Genna went, eager to hear what he had to say.

"You remember something about 'The Croft' then, Geoff?"

"I've been getting right paranoided about that blessed business. You'd think bobbies were listenin' round corner the way I've been goin' on."

After her experience with Issy at 'The Croft' Genna knew how he felt." She waited for him to go on.

"Y'see it were like this. Weren't I telling you about when I were a lad helping' me dad and there were something to do with porch at back of 'Croft' that were odd?"

"Yes, that was the bit you couldn't remember." Genna tried to be patient.

"Do you know when I walked round to that porch it all came *FLOODING BACK* to me, the sight of it all and the smell. It were smell I remembered as if it were yesterday." Geoff waved an informative arm around his head. "Tobacco smoke it were and them women never smoked a pipe."

"Tobacco smoke?" Genna wrinkled her nose.

"Aye, I'd stick me head round kitchen door, cheeky like and call, 'morning'…Just like I've been doin' for years at cottages round 'ere - passin' the time o' day, sociable, not that those two were ever sociable and Emily Gatenby got worse on her own."

"But you never SAW anyone smoking a pipe?"

"Na…but smell were as strong as a midden at times, just as though somebody had puffed a cloud and left suddenly. It must 'ave happened more than once for me to remember… then when I opened porch door and looked inside I remembered something else." The old man paused and screwed up his eyes.

"Go on, Geoff," Genna was getting impatient.

"I burnt me fingers on it! It were lying there on porch window bottom, a right beauty. I took hold to have a look an it were as hot as hell. Aye, it were a grand looking thing, bigger than the one me grandpa used to smoke."

"You actually saw a pipe?"

"Aye, but who the devil smoked it?. There were no gardener since ol' man Gatenby died, them two did it all themselves. There were no fella there at all!"

"How odd."

"A right fanciful tale, isn't it? I can't go and make a fool of mesen telling' them at bobby shop, can I? They'd think I were tryin' to make a bomb out of a damp squib."

"I can see what you mean." Genna was sympathetic.

"But then I laugh at what happened next. There were this rustlin'",Geoff wheezed with laugher, "I stepped back right hasty like and something large and grey shot past me ankles, like one of them horror movies…bloody yell… it were a rat, big as a

West Yorkshire bus, I'm not jokin' ...it could 'a'
been red and carried passengers."

Genna chortled with delight at his story but at
the same time thinking, firstly there had definitely
been a man living secretly at 'The Croft' and
secondly how quickly could she tell Issy about it?

As luck would have it Issy 'phoned just after
Genna arrived back at the farm.

"Just thought I've have a quick word, there are
things to report."

Genna made herself comfortable, it had been
known for Issy quick words to go on for half an
hour.

"I've been talking to John and just dropped in the
question of whether Summers and Goldthorpe had
been given the keys to 'The Croft'. We could then
have borrowed them and looked round the house
legitimately, taken our time without fear of being
disturbed, y'know, with the excuse William and
Debora might like it for when they're married or
something ridiculous like that." Issy gurgled with
laughter at the stupidity of such a likelihood, while
Genna cringed at the other end of the line.

"Anyway, John said the keys are still in the hands
of the solicitors, he knows because - now wait for
this - somebody has enquired about the house -
spotted it empty and wanted to look round.. This
guy was interested in development and wanted to
try and get planning permission! It is possible even
if you don't own the property. Can you believe it?"

"What's he want to build - high rise flats or a supermarket, they're very popular these days?"

"Genna, how could you even THINK of it? It IS almost as bad though. What he had in mind was a small static site - caravans, with the house in the centre, children's play area, the whole damn works. There's a lot of land if you imagine some of the trees cut down."

" Oh, Issy! That would mean endless visitors in your back yard."

"I hate to think. Father would have a fit, he sees enough of the public as it is but mother would love it."

"Now listen up a minute, you're not the only one with news." Genna went onto relate the story told to her by Geoff Cordingly which produced a deafening silence from Issy. "Well, for heavens sake, say something!"

"I'm completely stunned - we got it right, they were hiding somebody secretly who did not want to be seen, not even by the *milkman.*"

"Especially by the milkman!" He's the biggest gossip in the village, always has been, whatever age he was then."

"Good grief! Of course. You know what all this means?"

"It means we've got to make an attempt soon to get into the Rose room again and see if we can find anything before all this starts to happen."

"You bet. There is one thing, I have to visit the specialist next week to see how the leg's progressing. If it's going well I may be allowed out of plaster sooner that he thought which would make things a darn sight easier. I can't wait and John would be delighted."

Genna came off the phone looking pensive. Her mother caught the look. "Something on your mind, Gen?"

"No, not really, it's just that... it isn't possible to imagine how things could change but they could, couldn't they? Once they start you never know where they're going to end."

Jose frowned, obviously uncertain as to what she was getting at and quite aware that if she asked she probably wouldn't be told. "Thinking of running away, are we?"

"No. I'll be at the pub tonight same as usual." Genna smiled wryly and went off to tidy up in case William should put in an appearance. The day was not yet over.

CHAPTER FIFTEEN

The evening had been a disappointment with no sign of William, only the usual busy Saturday evening trade The sight of a light haired somebody in a navy T shirt had sent her spirits flying only to be flung to the floor when he turned round and was nothing like William. Once more Genna gave herself a dressing down for expecting too much. It was only dreams and for a while today she had allowed herself to forget reality.

It was late when she stepped out into the fresh night air. It smelt sweet and clean after the stuffy atmosphere of the pub. Better get used to that, as the weather improved it would be busier than ever on a Saturday, she reminded herself.

Nevertheless, it had been a good day for wages; Pete had given her extra for what had been longer sessions than normal but then, overall he'd never been mean when it came to paying her.

She crossed the cobbled yard serving as a car park for the pub and made her way to the farm truck. Looking up, she marvelled at the navy night sky as she had done many times before and though how something so simple could be so baffling; another of life's mysteries like the Rose room .

She recalled the pub yard had been occupied with vehicles when she had arrived earlier the same evening and she had not managed to park the truck on higher ground so that if it would not start she could roll it down the yard.

Five minutes later she was still sitting in the truck in exasperation having done her best to coax the engine into life. It heaved and grunted but there was no spark of life. It needed to be freewheeled some distance, thereby enabling her to slip it into gear but it would be impossible by herself. She glanced towards the backdoor of the pub wondering if there was anyone around to help, when a figure appeared.

"Are you stuck ,Gen?" Pete's voice called.

"Seems like it. The battery, it's been suspect for a while."

"Tell you what, leave it here for tonight. I'll drive you back. I'll get Dave to bring his leads out in the morning and give it a charge. Can you manage without it first thing?"

"I'll have to." Genna knew Dave who cooked the bar meals, tinkered with cars and had battery leads. He had not been there tonight as there was no proper catering, Saturday night drinkers took priority.

"I'll give you a bell first thing and see if he can drop them off."

"He won't be up. He doesn't have to get here until lunch time."

"Don't worry, Gen, I will be. I can go for them, he's only just down the village."

Pete, Genna noted, was certainly putting himself out to help. She suspected his motives but had no alternative short of walking in the dark.

"I'll go fetch the Range Rover keys," Pete called.

Genna wondered if he would tell his wife where he was going.

They were soon on their way to the farm. Neither spoke as they drove out of the now quiet village.

"It's about time that father of yours settled for a new truck, never mind a battery. That one could leave you stranded a long way from home." Pete broke the silence.

"I expect he will do one of these days." Genna was tired and felt little like making polite conversation. Pete on the other hand seemed full of energy.

"I reckon we had quite a day today. Did you see how that gang enjoyed themselves? Of course it's a big advantage having you behind the bar."

"You're a flatterer, Pete, but it won't get you anywhere, I can't do any more hours than I am at present."

"No, I'm serious, it makes a big difference having a pretty girl like you serving AND one who knows how to charming customers; that's the way they come back for more."

Genna closed her eyes and wished he would shut up. On the other hand he was her employer and it would not do to be churlish. "It doesn't take a lot of doing."

"How come you have no boyfriends hanging around on a Saturday night. Surely there must be somebody, some lad begging to take you out?"

Genna looked across at him, such a strong solid man. "There have been... lads, I suppose, just nobody I fancied." The reply was accompanied by a resigned shrug of her shoulders.

"Aye, you're right, girl, you're too good to be wasted on lads. What you need is a proper man." He chuckled, hands gripping the steering wheel competently as he negotiated a hairpin bend in the narrow road.

Genna hoped it did not mean how it sounded, like he was about to apply for the vacancy. She kept very quiet for the last stretch of the drive.

The rough track down to the farm was dark and bumpy but no great problem for the Range Rover. Pete pulled up opposite the yard gate.

"Thanks, Pete, that was good of you." Genna turned to the door. Pete sat silently looking across at her. The door did not seem easy to open.

"Doesn't the chauffeur get anything for his troubles?" His craggy face crinkled into a questioning smile and a big arm slid round the back of the seat giving an illusion of protective gentleness, certainly nothing she could really take offence at.

Genna realised she did not feel particularly intimidated, in fact she would not mind if he kissed her, the problem lay in where it may lead and she knew a plain 'no' was called for here and now.

The moment of indecision was a bad mistake and what's more Pete knew what he was doing to consolidate his progress as his arm eased her back into the seat. She was far from repulsed by Pete's embrace or his kiss. He had a clean fresh shirt smell, mixed faintly with aftershave and maleness. A half conscious question asked how he had managed that when he had been in the pub atmosphere all evening.

Somewhere in the back of her mind a voice reminded her this was the road to nowhere. She did not want somebody else's husband, never mind her fathers' cold scorn if any of it came to light.

A hand in her hair and the mouth exploring her own was chasing sensibility further away. Finger travelled silkily round her waist under her T shirt and stroked her back, his hands warm against her cold skin. She found herself moving against his big torso as he pulled her towards him. She realised that not only was she enjoying the experience but also the obvious pleasure it seemed to generate in him.

"Ah...Genna!"

Calling a halt was not what she had in mind at that moment, not that she had any set plan, except probably a short-lived snog from which she would withdraw herself in a way not to offend. Her lack of worldliness could be forgiven for although she had read about sex, she'd had little truly intimate experience and she was totally unprepared for what happened next.

To her amazement he suddenly sat back and hand to zip, produced something that in the dim light of the Range Rover she could only equate to the size and shape of a rolling pin, not a large rolling pin but one without its handle. Her next though were of his underpants, where were they?

Genna's mind went into scramble. She could see Issy helpless with laughter at her plight and she was pushing away the same reaction in herself. She bit her lip, whatever she did she must not laugh. She had no real time to dwell on the situation, his hand had taken hers and he was expecting her to hold the rolling pin, which, as it came into focus, she could see was warm flesh and blood.

"Go on, Gen, go on," he urged as she drew away.

It had all happened so quickly but surely she should have seen where it was leading. What on earth was she going to do? If she refused point blank to do as he asked he was easily big and strong enough to fight her into it... rape her even. A picture of Bobby Smailes came into her mind. What an idiot she was putting herself into the same situation she had been avoiding for long enough.

An arm around her shoulder tightened and made up her mind for her. If it was going to be rape she would have to fight.

"Pete! Stop!" She kept her voice calm even though she wanted to scream it at him.

At that moment fate, it appeared, had not decreed Genna should have more trouble that night. The sharp alarm raising bark of Fly filled the still night air. Her father would be out to see if there was a fox after the chickens should the sound continue.

"That's Fly raising the roof. It'll bring dad out any minute. I'd better go, Pete." She was amazed at how unflustered she sounded as she moved her hand to tuck in her top at the same time promising to exalt God for ever for rescuing her. She turned to Pete as she opened the door. "Just as well really, I might have had your missus after me with a twelve bore," she reminded him but keeping it light with a weather eye on the fact Pete had zipped his fly.

"Gen..." he held out his hand with a moan but it was obvious he had backed a loser.

DIARY NOTES
June 1943.

Gee is still in hospital . He is suffering from bouts of amnesia and there are times when we are talking he seems to drift off into another world but he always recognises me and they tell me he will be alright. The are sending him to convalesce for a period.

The awful bruising and lacerations have almost disappeared from his face but he still has a deep cut on his leg, although it is healing well. I will not be able to go and see him, it's too far but he has promised to write and he says he wants to get back flying and into the war, particularly as we are in a more hopeful position.

I am missing Gee so much. I still think about Rory and Tom but it is like a long ago dream. I was young and so innocent. I knew nothing of life or death. Nevertheless I am still left with the idea of

revenge after they gave away their young lives.
They were such pleasant young men. It spurs me on
to put up with the uncomfortable living conditions,
the worse food and all the other disciplines the
WAAF imposes each day.

The truth is Gee is the centre of my existence,
everything else is secondary. I spend my spare time
writing to him and praying that soon he will be fit
again.

Later, going over the incident with Pete in her
mind, Genna wondered if it would be an
inducement for him to sack her, probably on some
other pretext. On further thought she came to the
conclusion she had hardly dished out any big
rejection but had initially returned his amorous
overtures. Circumstances had curtailed things from
getting further out of hand (or was it 'in' hand'.)
She smiled to herself.

Of course this brought round the fact that, given
the opportunity, he would try again. She would
have to make a stand and apologise for giving him
the wrong impression before this happened. If only
it could have been William....

There was simply one thing to do: when Pete
arrived next morning with the truck she would put
him right, tell him... tell him what? She really like
him but there was no way she felt she could
become involved. She would have to be firm or
there would be a repeat performance. On the
other hand if she were rude, he may find an excuse

to sack her. It needed handling very carefully. She went to sleep trying to solve the problem.

As things turned out it was Dave, who, on Saturday morning, appeared driving the truck. "I've charged the battery, Gen, and cleaned the plugs, just tweaked it a bit and it's running a treat. Pete's seen me right - he says he has to look after his employees and you rely on it for work. Can you drop me back in Elvingdale?"

"Of course I can," she told him, thanking him, knowing he would have missed his Sunday's lie in and wondering with a nagging doubt about Pete's generosity, not to mention free lunches that never were.

CHAPTER SIXTEEN

It was 10:30 am. When Genna found herself in Elvingdale and early for the pub's midday session. There was no real point in returning home and for once she had time on her hands.

Bessie's for coffee sounded like the best bet and after dropping Dave she parked the truck at the pub and headed for the tea shop. Bessie, in flowered overall and the usual headscarf, was bustling around and pleased to see her.

At first Genna did not spot the newspaper hiding its reader in the far alcove of the café; apart from two elderly ladies, she had though the place empty. When the newspaper came down she saw John Glendenning, smiling a welcome and beckoning her to join him.

"My favourite pastime, coffee and papers on a Sunday morning." His attractive grin, dark hair tousled as usual, made him a pleasant prospect for a chat.

"How's the property market this week, no developers taking over the place?"

Genna fished as she sat down at his table. She trusted Issy enough to believe she had kept quiet about their involvement at 'The Croft.'

"No, but my situation has just had a rock dropped on it - well depending how you look at it, I suppose"

Genna raised an enquiring eyebrow wondering if it was anything that would affect Issy.

"It's quite a tale actually. Are you in a rush?"

Genna assured him that for once in her life she was not.

"The family's solicitor has contacted me to tell me my grandfather has died suddenly."

Genna shot him a sympathetic look as he went on.

"Yes, he lived up in Scotland way up towards the Highlands where he was the local laird - lived in a castle and owned acres of land, and ... I happen to be his heir. Anyway, this legal guy was getting twitchy, mother's in America playing golf, dad slipped of the dish some time ago, and the funeral's next week and of course, I should be there, especially as he has not managed to contact mother."

"Heavens, John, you mean you may be joining the landed gentry?"

"It's interesting - shooting, fishing rights, pine forest by the ton. I believe the old man's let things go a bit but, for me it's manna from heaven - just my thing."

"That's so brilliant for you. What's Issy's take on it?" To Genna's surprise John's face fell and he ran a distracted hand through his hair.

"Actually I haven't told her yet, there's a sort of snag...but..."

At that moment Bessie arrived with a large pot of coffee and a plate of biscuits. "Good to see folk relaxin' for once. She gave Genna a meaningful stare. Young un's don't stop to smell roses on the way." She left them muttering that life was just one take and not a bloody rehearsal.

John smiled wryly and poured the coffee. "It'll be more than one take if I tell Issy what's happened. Look, Gen, don't breathe a word to her but I'm having trouble... with one of the staff. I know I can trust you.."

Genna had a fair idea whose name he was about to say.

"It's Leonie, she's positively stalking me." John ladled sugar absent- mindedly into his cup. " She waits until I'm in the office alone and she wears this pelmet ... she bends down to the bottom draw in the filing cabinet just next to my desk and she's barely any knickers on and the legs...Oh God! I go dizzy..."

"Would I take her to the 'Pirates of Penzance' was the next thing. Somebody had given her tickets for Saturday. I made excuses I'm reading to my maiden aunt and she fixes me with those damn light blue eyes as though she believes me, then proceeds to bump into me with tits that stick out like the proverbial chapel hat pegs. She's driving me up the wall." John held his head and groaned quietly after the outpouring.

Genna could hardly think of a thing to say. One thing was certain, if Issy got word of such a scenario she would be plotting an early death for Leonie.

"I'm being Christopher Robin, would you believe, as good as can be, never encouraged her and what with Issy having the pot... you know, Genna, self-help is not my answer!"

He said it with such feeling, Genna, despite herself , found she had her head down and was laughing helplessly at his plight. "John ... sorry, it's not really funny for you but something similar happened to me lately...no, I can't tell you but I can appreciate only too well how it is."

"Look, Genna, this wasn't the end of it, (more hair raking). He lent towards her and lowered his voice. "Honestly, Genna, it's something I can't talk to Issy about but maybe you could give me some advise - you're so level headed and you know what Issy's like."

"If you knew what a mess my own life is you might not be so quick to say that."

Genna smiled wryly, "but of course I'll help if I can."

"Right, I told the office I would not be there next week because I have to go to Scotland for a funeral on Tuesday. Leonie shrieked and said it was her mother's birthday and SHE hoped to go to Scotland - Stirling, by train and how marvellous, I would be able to give her a lift, wouldn't I? It's on the way. I couldn't think of a bloody thing to say - she'll be planning to eat me!"

Genna remembered the wife in Kettlington and how John had felt sorry for her. He was obviously a softie at heart but Leonie was already on Issy's hit list for telling her about that episode; it would spell big trouble if she got a whiff of John taking Leonie to Scotland.

"You see, Genna if some girl came on to me and she was okay I'd just ...well...give in ... you know, think of England or rather Scotland." He smiled sheepishly. "It was all a breeze but now I don't want to do that, I want Issy properly - a one way ticket."

Genna nodded, liking him more by the minute. "It may be best not to say anything and hope she doesn't find out. She'll just natter herself about it. On the other hand you could tell the truth - say what a damn nuisance Leonie is and you don't have much choice."

"Oh God! That sounds best but she'll go spare!"

At that moment the café door opened and to Genna's delight she saw William walking across to them. As he drew closer the pair could see a dark blue weal under his left eye.

"Thought I might find you here, John."

"Wills, what the hell...?" John started.

"Oh, nothing much, just a monumental row with Debora. It seems she can get rough when she's mad. Women!" He pulled a chair out beside them and looked across at Genna. "I'm not including dark haired ones with blue eyes."

Genna smiled, conscious of her knees changing their structure.

"Join the Lonely Hearts Club?" John chuckled waving a hand at himself and Genna. "The course of true love is going zigzag round here. Genna's plagued by the opposite sex too, so you're in good company."

Genna did not know whether to kill him or kiss him, here mind was dancing on the ceiling. One thing was assured, whatever Saturday night's revelations may have held, Sunday morning's were making them look like a tea party.

DIARY NOTES
1943, September.

Gee is much better and about to go back to his squadron. There is real hope now that the battle of the Atlantic has turned in our direction. The Germans are not gaining ground as they were. Russian manpower is holding out even though so many of them have been slaughtered. We must win. I believe we will and Gee and I will have a future together.

October.

Although he appears to be quite well and he is back flying, Gees letters leave me wondering. His writing has changed and he is not as self-assured. I think at times he suffers from some kind of melancholy. When we meet he is quiet. He does not talk as freely, or as much as he used to. On the other hand he seems to rely on me more than ever as a comfort and a source of strength, which I am more than willing to try and be.

I am suspicious that he has been hiding his misgivings about his mental strength from the doctors. I saw him put on a brave face, a more robust front when they were around.

I have been moved further south. I had better not say where. I had a forty-eight hour pass and was able to spend it with Gee in London. He knows his way around so well even though there are yawning, toothless gaps in the streets.

He wanted me to go with him to meet his parents but that was where I turned coward and in the end I refused. He went by himself and I waited for him at the hotel. We booked in as Mr. And Mrs. G. Wade and left out the Bigham. Everything was marvellous, just as it used to be, until the time came for him to return to camp. It was though a shadow came over him. He sat morosely looking into space. Something is not quite right.

December.

I don't know what to do about the latest development. In his last letter Gee told me he did not want to fly any more. He does not even want to be in the RAF. He says, and I'm not really surprised, it has been building up for some time. I have told him to see his MO. But he argues it will mean admitting to cowardice and simply being scared of dying, like everyone else. He says physically there is nothing wrong with him; he cannot bear the though of all this slaughter as a result of the bombing. He does not seem to be facing the reality of what he should do.

There is a short term solution: we both have some

leave which we could arrange to take at the same time. I am going to take him home. The break from it all in the Dales may be just what he needs. I have told him how quiet it is and right away from the war. He seems to really like the idea.

As it turned out neither William or John gave out any further information about their respective romantic dilemmas as they sat over coffee in the tea shop. Both appeared to avoid the subject as far as Genna could see.

John's position, which involved William's sister, made this understandable and no doubt, Genna concluded, William was embarrassed about the black eye. Details of the charity day and other incidents to do with the pub were covered and Genna was once more made aware of the way he looked at her, of the warmth between William and herself.

Reluctantly she said her goodbyes and dragged herself away from their company. It was time for her to go to the pub.

She was at the entrance to the snicket where old Mrs. Clarke lived when, who should appear, but the lady herself coming towards her. Genna called good morning and stopped to talk to her.

"I right enjoyed our cuppa tea other day and I were thinkin' if there wert anything else I could remember about 'Croft.' Talkin about it an' all I could just see Emmy Gatenby all over ag'in and how she used to sit and write to them boys, spent hours at it she did."

"You did say she was only a young girl then. Somebody in the village mentioned she'd gone into the WAAF. In the war. Is that right?"

"Aye, that were what I was about to tell you. Knew there was summat else, something I remember my sister said. You would have liked our Maud - real bright spark she were, bit of a one for the men, bless her. She's gone to her maker has Maud..." Mrs. Clarke lifted her eyes solemnly to heaven as though Maud might be looking down.

Genna waited patiently while thoughts were directed to Maud and hoped she wouldn't be late for the pub.

"Our Maud were younger than me and in t'war she did a bit for old Mrs. Gatenby when Emmy were in the WAAF. Emmy used to come home on leave and our Maud said, just as I told you, she were always writing to somebody."

"You mean the cousins who used to come and stay?" Genna frowned.

"Don't think it were them boys, summat happened to them, not right certain what, maybe they were killed in the war. Blessed if I can remember who it were she wrote to. Maybe Maud didn't cotton on to that - not as sharp as me y'know. Any road Maud didn't work very long owin' to the fact she got pregnant but I do remember her sayin' what with the journal Emmy wrote and them letters, she never had a chance to talk to her much like I used to."

"Journal?"

"Aye, never let it out of her sight, Scared to death she were, her mother might read it. Maud knew about it because I told her; we used to gossip about Emmy and how she used to hide stuff from her mother. I remember Maud telling' me Emmy left the journal behind her one day as she went out of the room and Maud followed her and gave it to her. She made a right fuss o' Maud for doing that. Funny how you clean forget until something comes along and opens a little door in y' mind. I can see Maud telling' me that as though she were standing beside me... sayin' as how she wouldn't want her mother to read it."

Genna felt a shiver come over her as she watched the old lady visit the past and the company of her sister. "You mean a journal like a diary?"

"Aye, that's it. Don't know what the devil it were all about. Some secret fella' me lad, I suppose. We wouldn't snoop like that me and Maud." Mrs. Clarke's chin rose in the air.

Surely, Genna pondered, if the diary was so important, Emily Gatenby may have kept it, not in the house but hidden in the Rose room.

She left Mrs. Clarke and made her way quickly to the pub dreading the prospect of facing Pete. Nearing 'The Unicorn' she could feel herself becoming more nervous about what she had to say to him.

The obvious thing would be to apologise and make it sound as if he had been fooled into thinking he could go ahead. Something like 'Sorry I gave out the wrong vibes last night, Pete. It was my fault and it won't happen again.' That may keep her job safe and the important wages coming in. But why the devil should she apologise? Was it really her fault? Maybe it was best to ignore the whole issue and act as though nothing had happened.

She reached the pub with no clear idea of what action to take. When she arrived in the bar Pete was in the back and called out to her in his usual friendly fashion.

"Hi, Genn. That truck alright this morning, was it?"

"Simply brilliant and thanks a lot for getting Dave to fix it. By the way, Pete, I think we had our wires cross..." She started. Pete was shaking his head ever so slightly and then lifted a cautionary finger to his lips. Genna almost jumped as a slight figure appeared out of the back, his wife no less.

"Morning, Genna, we're stuck for extra help today, so if it's busy you'll have me to rely on."

Genna's mouth was dry and she knew she said something about how that would be great, at the same time thinking maybe his wife was more clued into Pete's roving ways than he imagined and had her own devices for keeping him in check. One thing was certain it had solved Genna's problems with him for the immediate future.

She found herself again thinking about William as she pulled pints. She did not really want to dwell on his fight with Debora. What good would that do, they could make it up in no time? Even so it would be interesting to know what had prompted her to give him a black eye.

She arranged to see Issy when she came to the pub on Monday evening. She may know what had happened and have a chance to tell her. More importantly they must try and fix another illicit visit to 'The Croft' to see if they could find something that looked like a journal tucked away in some hidden corner; that surely would help them find answers to the question of the body.

CHAPTER SEVENTEEN.

The weather was still fine and dry. The warm
spell showed no inclination of going away. The
conditions agreed with the sheep and their lambs
but the next problem would be to ensure they had
enough water. There were still ewes to lamb and
with those already milking, they needed a good
deal of fluid, or their milk would grow sparse.

The gutters and the ditches of the high moorland
could dry out with the sun and a moisture zapping
wind. The sheep may have to be moved elsewhere.
The visitors saw only the lambs frisking and
chasing, the brightness and beauty of it all.

For a Monday evening the pub was busy. Issy
came in as quickly as the pot would allow and
found herself a stool tucked into the corner of the
bar. Genna was busy serving but managed a quick
hello.

"John's grandfather's died and he has to go to
Scotland," Issy hissed as John followed her over.
"Tell you about it later."

Genna nodded wondering if John had given her
the full version, or the abridge edition. John winked
at her as he ordered drinks, whatever that meant.
Obviously it would be best to say as little as
possible of their Sunday conversation at the tea
room.

Not long afterwards William appeared wearing
discreetly tinted glasses. There was a lull in trade
and their heads turned to talk to Genna as she

served his drink.

"I believe we are about to have a Monarch of the Glen amongst us, kilt and all." Issy announced in a pseudo Scotts accent, giving John a quirky look.

"I bumped into Genna on Sunday and gave her a quick resume of the situation." John glanced meaningfully at Genna who remained silent.

"William's been fighting too." Issy appeared determined to stir everyone up.

"Issy! For heavens sake! I shall be glad when that pot comes off and you arrive home tired like the rest of us and not fizzing with suppressed energy."

"Oh, sorry, Mr. Doctor, hush my big mouth. Talk to John for a bit and leave me to let of steam to Genna." Issy turned impatiently away from her brother and William seemed relieved to do as she suggested.

"The eye, Genna murmured, "do you know what happened?"

Issy bent further over the bar and murmured back. "A right old tale. Do you remember an Ian Sykes who John told me he had seen with Debora in Leeds? Well, Debora is always carping at William because he's never there when it's her day off. He cannot help it, that's a doctor's lot - patients first, especially when he's trying to prove himself in the practice."

Genna nodded, at the same time trying to keep her mind on pulling a pint for a customer positioned further down the bar. Issy continued.

"It seems she threw it at William that Ian Sykes

could always find a way of being there for her however much photography work he had on... then it came out she'd been using Ian as a stop-gap!" Issy paused as Genna took money from the customer and then gave her full attention to what Issy was saying.

"William was fed up with all this and told her to jigger off to Ian, if that was how far her integrity went, or words to that effect. Debora was furious and clouted him."

"He's broken off the engagement?" Genna asked, her heart doing a quick sprint around her chest.

"He didn't say so, just that he was right off women. Don't you fancy him, Gen?"

"Like mad, me and six hundred others. Chance would be a big deal." The question had taken her by surprise but she made light of it, not risking the drama Issy would love. "But listen to this, I saw old Mrs. Clarke today." Genna deftly changed the subject keeping her voice even lower. "She says Emily Gatenby kept a journal - you know, a diary. My guess is, it could be hidden in the Rose room because she wasn't likely to leave it lying around the house, she wanted to keep it secret from her mother. Mrs. Clarke's sister, Maud, knew all about that."

Issy's eyes turned to delighted saucers. "Perhaps that will really spill the beans! Great! When are we visiting? I see the ortho man tomorrow morning ... may even have the pot off. Can you go tomorrow afternoon?"

The rest of the evening for Genna was frittered away with serving customers. She dried glasses dismally afterwards, hoping Pete would not return early from The Fell Rescue meeting and unhappy she had not exchanged one word with William.

The outcome of the orthopaedic appointment was not quite how Issy had hoped. The pot had been exchanged for a long back slab bandaged on from thigh to ankle and when Genna arrived at 'The Rectory' the next day Issy appeared distracted and unhappy.

"You okay?" She enquired of Issy.

"I am SO NOT happy. I'll tell you about it on the way. I though we could take it slowly and walk, which means I can take Fifi and also nobody will know we are there like they did before."

Issy levered herself down the stone steps of 'The Rectory' with the help of a walking stick, followed by Fifi, eager to be off. The two girls set off slowly down the drive through the gates and turned right up the lane towards 'The Croft.'

The trees were now becoming thick with new leaves arching hoop-like over their heads. At the high side of the lane the roots appeared as bulging woody veins disappearing into the long grass. The boxer bitch bounded happily ahead of them snuffling and snorting into dank ditches where she considered there would be rabbit holes. The smell of the dank earth brought back memories of digging and remains and Genna shivered partly at the memory and also because they may find conclusive facts about the body.

"Something mega dreadful must have happened, you haven't said a word for five minutes," she told Issy.

"I can hardly cope with thinking about it."

"What, for heaven's sake?"

"That man-eater in the estate agents - Leonie, she's gone to Scotland with John."

"Did John tell you that?"

"No, I went into the village with mother first thing and saw John's car. John came out and Leonie followed him. She got into the car with a hold all"

Things were bad, Genna decided; Issy had found out in the worst possible way. She would have to say something to Issy but how, without breaking John's confidence to her?

"I thought maybe they were just going to Kettlington and John would call back before he set off for Scotland so I went in and asked the other girl. She took great delight in telling me Leonie had gone to Scotland with John and guess what?"

"What?"

"She'd forgotten her nightie but she didn't think she'd need it with John to keep her warm!"

"OH, GOD! Listen, Issy when I saw John on Sunday he happened to say he was really serious about you and Leonie had been pestering the life out of him for a lift to Scotland and what a damn nuisance she was." (*So much for confidences.*)

"Well, she got what she wanted, didn't she?"

Issy's brain then managed to take over from her emotions. "Did he really say he was serious? Why on earth didn't he tell me about Leonie?"

"Maybe he thought you would go into the estate agents with an axe."

"You're right - I WOULD!" Issy managed a small laugh at herself.

"There you're... he was being sensible, he doesn't want Leonie"

"No, but Genna, she wants him - his body! He admits he's always enjoyed women and he's been practically celibate for weeks."

"I hope he doesn't revert to wearing his kilt or he'll have no price of escaping!" Both girls laughed. The crisis receded to Genna's relief as Issy lightened up.

The progress was slow as the two walked and talked. Genna did her best to reassure Issy but she found her mind wandered to the lonely solitude of the lane as they drew nearer to 'The Croft.' They were surrounded by a sea of Cow Parsley, the masses of tiny frothy flowers making a heady floral champagne on both sides of the lane.

Genna could see a picture of a girl riding, solitary and determined along the same route, the horse stepping carefully up through the same arched trees, the same flowers, her father dead, her mother a heavy shadow in her life. What had happened to turn Emily Gatenby into such a loner as she grew older?

DIARY NOTES.
Christmas, 1943.

Christmas was a very happy time. Gee seemed to settle well, although the three of us had very little company other than our own. The quietness and the character of the Dales away from the war appeared to agree with him totally. He did not start with the headaches until two days before we were due back and they became worse and worse, then something unbelievable happened.

He said he did not want to go back to camp. I begged him to do so and then see his MO. He replied that if we would let him stay he was going to go AWOL as nobody would know where he was; it is, after all, quite remote here.

All this seems so out of character for George but what can I do? He will not go sick. He says he will be called a coward trying to get out when there is nothing physically wrong and he cannot face that. He knows his father would be appalled.

I should have said, the strangest part of this is that mother is on his side. She took to him like a long lost son and he can do no wrong. I never imagined this would be the case. I know his dark good looks are so appealing and his lovely smile but it is his quietness too, mother likes and, I suppose his background and well informed, bookcase mind. As far as she is concerned I picked a winner. She says he can use father's old hideaway. Because of the panelling door nobody will know he is there, even if they come looking for him.

I cannot believe she does not understand...or maybe she does understand and wants him totally dependent on us, like I used to be on her. If he does go back maybe she imagines I could somehow lose him and this is the surest way for it to work out so this would not happen.

Dear God! I just go round in circles. I don't know what to think or do. He says he has left no indication of his true whereabouts. Both he and I have moved about. He has been out of the way in hospital and we have never been ones to talk of our relationship. I have been secretive as always. Nobody is going to look here.

He tells me I must go back and say nothing about him being here. I know I shall be a hopeless liar if I'm asked but I love my darling Gee so much and I loath to see him troubles and unhappy.

The last night before I left him we made love. He does not seem as capable as he used to be but in the end it was marvellous and we were practically sobbing in each others arms.

It was after this that he confined to me that a week before he came away he actually phoned his mother and told her he may not come back. He seems closer to her than any other member of the family. (He has a younger sister too.) he did not tell his mother where he would be going only that she may not hear from him for a long time and not to worry. He must have thought about this idea quite

*seriously. She immediately sent him a package and
a note which he showed to me.*

*Willow Park Mansions,
Mayfair,
LONDON.*

16TH December, 1943.

*My Dear Gee,
I am so sorry to hear what you have to tell me,
darling, but you must do whatever you feel best for
yourself. We all have our own destinies to work
out. I shall of course not tell your father, he simply
would not understand these things as you and I do.*

*I know you would not ask me for it but I enclose
ready cash. You are so dear to me, I have sent all I
have available, about £250.*

*What I am sending, which will eventually be of
more use when we come through this ghastly war,
is some of my jewellery of which I have so much.
There may be a time when you will need to dispose
of it. It could be worth quite a penny or two, so be
discreet. I would prefer you to have it than it should
sit here being useless as it is at the moment,
(entertaining is not what it used to be.) If you father
should miss these things, you know what an eagle
eye he has, I shall tell him they must have been
stolen, (maids can be very light fingered.)*

*I do so hope you will be alright, my darling, I shall
think of you. Let me know if you can.*

Your ever adoring,

Mama.

The entry into 'The Croft' was dramatised by Fifi who clattered up the bare stairs and began snuffling along the skirting board in the region of the Rose room. She looked up startled as though hearing something at the other end of the corridor and then continued snorting and sniffing.

"We should have brought her the last time. She knows exactly where the room is without a search." Genna commented as she waited for Issy to reach the top of the stairs.

The room appeared lighter than on the previous visit, nevertheless, Genna went quickly to open the window as Issy looked around.

"The bureau, Gen, that's where we may find something." The bureau was duly tried and found to be locked.

"The key's sure to be somewhere here. People usually do shove keys into the nearest thing they can find. We'll have to hunt." Genna picked up a small ornament jug and peered inside to no avail.

When they came to the mantelpiece and a 1920s Art Deco ornament their search was rewarded as Issy tipped two small keys out onto the table in the window.

"Look one's bigger, let's try that." She gave it to Genna who stepped towards the bureau and pushed the key into the lock. It turned easily revealing a row of pigeon holes stuffed with letters and papers.

"Grief! It'll take us hours to sift through this lot." Issy moaned.

"Yes, but...we can easily spot a diary, it's sure to be thicker, come on, help me look."

It was, as Genna said, but ten minutes was enough to prove there was no book to spot, only a lot of old bills and household correspondence.

"We should have known it wouldn't be that easy."

"Wait a minute what about this drawer in the middle?" Genna gave the drawer a tug. It appeared to be stuck and she pulled harder. "There's something jamming inside."

Bit by bit the draw gave just enough for her to push in her fingers and press down on the offending contents. The drawer slid open.

"It's a sort of velvet pouch - look it's buttoned down." Issy gave it a half heartened poke.

"Let's see what's inside." Genna unfastened the velvet button and tipped out the contents onto the pulled down desk top lid.

"Just our luck...grubby old costume jewellery, necklaces, rings, brooches, you name it." Issy pushed the pile around separating the contents.

"I wonder if those are diamonds in this car brooch and what about this snake choker, it looks like gold...and the eye, look at the eye, a ruby?" Genna murmured.

"I like the leopard brooch - definitely all diamonds!" Issy chortled.

At that moment there was a loud crescendo of barks from the corridor. Both girls looked up in dismay.

"Not the police AGAIN?" Issy limped over to the window. "No sign of a car."

Genna went into the corridor followed by Issy. Fifi, back legs splayed and hackles standing up, was growling menacingly while looking down the corridor appearing to see something invisible to their eyes.

"Do you think that dog senses a ghost - dogs can, it's like a seventh sense?" Issy grabbed Genna's arm.

"Shh... I can hear something... listen" Genna waited, head on one side. The noise could be described as a muffled bump and a series of small knocks coming from the end of the corridor, sending Fifi into another angry series of growls and barks. "It's a clumsy sort of ghost, if you ask me." Genna muttered.

"Come on, let's put that stuff back and get out of here. I'm not ready to meet Emily Gatenby's spirit yet."

Genna decided maybe Issy had a point - better to play safe, as again they made a hasty departure from The Croft.

It was as they were retreating down the drive that Genna turned to look at the house as she had done before. "OH, God! Issy, we've forgotten to close the window… I'll have to go back. If the police are around they could easily spot somebody had been in and they'll start surveillance. Stay here. You'll never make it with that leg."

"Genna, I'm so sorry to be useless, you're so capable and I'm a wash out. Look, if there's anything up there, just yell from the window and I'll come back up if it kills me. Take Fifi, she's really protective."

It was with some dread that Genna went back into the house, Fifi following her. Both girl and dog stopped at the bottom of the staircase. Fifi looked up and back at Genna questioningly. "Come on, Fifi, it's got to be done"

The corridor was quiet as they went back into the Rose room. The two keys were sitting on the table. Genna shut the window and waved to Issy. Just as she was asking herself where the other key could possibly fit, more noise could be heard from outside the room and Fifi was once more giving voice to a volley of barks. This was ridiculous, Genna told herself and whatever it may be there was no such things as ghosts. She wished she was quite sure. With a firm hand on the dog's collar she tiptoed down the corridor, her heart ready to scramble out of her chest at the smallest provocation.

The sound appeared to be coming from the bathroom. She lay her hand on the door knob. There was complete silence as she turned the knob slowly and peered through the crack. There, in the middle of the bathroom stood a large pigeon, purple grey feathers ruffled and head on one side, looking towards the noise. She exhaled a great sigh and went in, shutting the door after her to keep out an eager Fifi.

Liberating a bird from inside a room through the window was no great problem to Genna, she could deal with it as easily as she could skin a rabbit. The window was just a fraction open at the top and pushed down with some persuasion. The bird flew happily towards the trees and Genna thought how simple life was when one's fears were confronted.

Just how the bird came to be in the bathroom was not something she stayed to investigate, as she explained to Issy when they walked back down the drive. "Perhaps a hole in the roof, Issy offered. You were dead brave to go back. I was scared to death for you."

"When I was in that room I just had another thought... an idea about the other key." Issy shot her an enquiring look while hanging onto Genna's arm.

"Both keys were on the table and the only other keyhole I could see was in the little cupboard over the mantelpiece. Maybe, Issy, just maybe, the diary could be in that cupboard. Tell you what though, I'm not risking my chances back there again today but we must and soon."

CHAPTER EIGHTEEN

Genna's school pick ups in the minibus were in fairly normal form. They were mostly a group of seven to ten year olds but for the last two afternoons the group had been smaller because the boys had been involved in the school's tug of war team leaving Genna to ferry the younger girls.

One or two of the girls tended to curry her favour and they all loved a giggle. It was not surprising when one of the younger ones chirped up with new information.

"Miss, I know what a lesbian is, my mum says it's girls who don't have boy friends, they just like girls. You have a girl friend, are you a lesbian, Miss?" The giggles were heavily smothered.

"No, Julie, I'm not a lesbian and it's a *bit* more complicated than that".

"Yes, I know my mum says sometimes the get their jeans muddled up but how does this happen if they're not in the wash together?"

"It's not easy to explain, it's nothing to do with the jeans you wear. You'll have to ask your mum more about it when you get older."

It was all fairly routine stuff, leaving them chattering about genes and jeans but Genna felt taken aback. Was this what they thought in the village, no boyfriends and therefore she was probably a lesbian? She swerved to avoid a cat who was about to cross in front of her. She reminded herself to keep her mind on the job as she managed to avoid the animal. If word got round she was of such a persuasion, no promising male in the village, not that many, would look in her direction. The worst of it was William, suppose he got wind of such gossip. The thought was too catastrophic to imagine.

She dropped off the children at the village centre making sure each and every child was taken care of. The next stop was the garage to swap the minibus for the farm truck. There was barbed wire to pick up on the way home and various small items from the ironmongers but that would not take long; the store was on the way out of the village.

She climbed back into the truck hoping the battery would behave itself after Dave's treatment on Sunday morning. The God's were smiling, the truck started sweetly and she set off for the homeward run.

She was not far from her objective, at least onto farm land when, coming round the bend she was confronted by a herd of sheep straggling ahead down the narrow lane and busily cropping the grass on the verge. Her Father's brand marks were plain to see. Further down the road Genna spotted the telltale gap from where they had escaped. The wall had tumbled and the sheep had grabbed the chance of sweeter grass on the other side.

She pulled up with a lurch as a sheep ran unexpectedly into the radiator. The truck gave a shudder that did not sound healthy. Genna got out to try and herd the sheep back towards the gap in the wall. It would have been easier to catch treacle. No sooner were a few retrieved than the first lot wandered out again. There was only one solution, to go on up to the farm and collect Fly so that the dog could round them up.

Back in the truck she tried to start the engine. It heaved a few turns expectantly and then went dead. Genna's heart sank at the realisation the battery had gone flat yet again. She was still at least a mile from the farm and there would be all the more time for the sheep to spread the word and do a mass exit. There was nothing to do but walk.

She was just about to lock the door and set off when a large estate car came round the bend finding its way through the less determined of the sheep. She stepped out of its way beside the truck and the estate car pulled up alongside almost wedging her between the two vehicles. William smiled at her from behind the wheel.

"You appear to have no means of escape. Has it got sheep up its carburettor or just conked?"

"It's the battery again... it's driving me nuts. I stopped for the sheep and the darn thing won't start. I'll have to fetch the dog and get this lot back in."

"I've been to see your mother but hop in and I'll drive you back. I was hoping you'd be at home but now we can talk on the way."

"You have a lovely habit of appearing at just the

right moment." Genna shot him a grateful, smiling look.

William was dressed quite formally in dark trousers and a white shirt, his tie and a jacket were on the back seat. He was still wearing the tinted glasses almost covering his cheek bone which sported a faint variety of bruise colours.

All in all for Genna, he had to be her modern day Sir Galahad but, unfortunately, not the knight sporting Angenna McFaiden's colours, she reminded herself.

"Your mother seems to be doing very well with the new regime." William sat back and glanced at her as she settled herself beside him in the car."

"She's certainly much better. I am so relieved about her."

"As far as I'm concerned, she is still well underweight and it would be advisable for her to take life a lot easier."

"There is always so much physical work to do on a farm, apart from the garden and any domestic stuff. How is it possible to persuade her to stop?" Genna held her hands out in a helpless gesture. "I wish I knew."

Mmm...you don't exactly sit around all day. I expect she's asking herself who'll get the extra jobs and would feel guilty when she knew it would be you. No doubt your father's a workaholic too?"

"He's quite single minded. I'm afraid I'm the one who could be sidetracked, there are so many other things I would like to do."

William's half smile made his eyes crinkled encouragingly behind the glasses , inviting her confidence. "Go on, tell me about it. What would you rather be doing?"

Genna was about to open her mouth to pour out all her secret longings, then stopped herself. The sheep were out and wandering further a field; she should be back collecting Fly. It was important the livestock be cleared from the road. She settled for a compromise. "I want to finish my education, study, and if possible gain qualifications... before I settle down - you know get married." (That would be a rumour stopper.)

"But simple things are important too, like reading and music. There's no chance in that direction. I should be fetching the dog right now." She turned anxiously to look at the road and the sheep straggling ahead.

"Sure." William started his car and proceeded to find his way through the sheep.

"Genna glanced momentarily at his eye wondering if she dare ask, at the same time not sounding too nosey. Of course she dare. Go for it she told herself. "Your eye still looks sore. Have you made friends with Debora?"

"You mean my ex fiancé? We have decided to go our separate ways."

"William, I'm sorry it's gone wrong." Genna lied.

"It must have been pretty traumatic." She realised she sounded so cool when in reality the elation inside her swelled, about to explode into a thousand stars at the fact that he was free.

"In some ways it's a weight off my shoulders." William stated very deliberately. "At first it was that trip to the moon on gossamer wings but I came crashing down to reality just in time, I'm glad to say."

While inside Genna glowed with the secret joy, she felt ashamed at how two faced she could be but she went on daring herself, making things happen. "Are you coming into the pub tonight?"

"Early, if I can, depending on the surgery. We could have a chat before it gets too busy. Issy's not out - some sorrow she's not sharing, to do with John, I suppose."

So Issy was still brooding. It slipped to the side of her mind as Genna felt once more the unfamiliar surge of happiness, like hot water bottle found in a cold bed. She mentally tried to shrug it off. She mustn't get used to that, it would be too hard to do without it.

DIARY NOTES.
June, 1944.

Summer has arrived with the most wonderful news - 'D' Day 6th. June, the Allies landed on the coast of Normandy. We are going to come out alive and on the winning side.

Mother writes that Gee is not too bad. He has headaches that come and go. He sits and smokes his pipe as though in a world apart from reality, often in the hideaway. She gives him meals and sees him at the Rose window looking out over the village. She thinks he reads on good days but he says little and she is not one to probe into other people's lives.

Nobody has officially questioned me about him which is just as well. Maybe he told them he was going home. There are so many people lost in the war, ones that disappear without trace, especially in the London bombing. The authorities simply cannot account for everyone killed in air raids. Some poor souls are just blown apart.

Gee has always played his cards close to his chest, just like I do. There is always the possibility he cooked something up with his mother and she threw out a red herring for him, saying he was coming home to London and he never arrived. The tone of her letter makes me wonder.

NOVEMBER, 1944

It should son be over now. I could be demobbed next year. I have just been home. Gee was so much thinner and appears to have retreated into himself. Although he was pleased to see me and he confined to me of how he had nightmares, he has somehow taken a step back from reality.

It makes me very sad to think I have somehow lost him. The wonderful man I loved so much is not quite there any more. It is a mystery to me how he is able to stay in the Dales for almost a year and not take part in life. He has changed so much. Unbelievably, mother has accepted it, she seems to understand what he has been through almost to the extent that I do.

When it came to being close he seemed uncertain about making love to me. I encouraged him. At last it worked and was nearly as beautiful as it used to be, although it was difficult to make it complete but eventually it was. I just wish he would go and see a doctor and get back to his old self. There is something wrong with his mental state and it stems from the head injury and the spell of concussion. I'm sure there could be treatment for this.

Genna returned home to find her mother resting on the old sofa in the kitchen. The minute she spotted her daughter she made to get up to put on the kettle.

"Mum, stay put, I can do it. I've just seen William and he was saying how important it is you should do less and put on weight."

"Genna, William may be a first rate doctor and a compassionate young man but he does NOT know a damn thing about running a Yorkshire hill farm in times such as these when the area's been affected by a foot and mouth epidemic. Just when I'm feeling better - do less indeed, I should be doing more."

Genna made a cup of tea and tried a different tack. "The news from the market is the lamb prices are on the up and things generally are going better. Couldn't we think of extra help? Maybe you could talk it over with dad and tell him you need to rest."

Her mother's jaw tightened. "We talked about it the other day. I reminded him what an intelligent, thoughtful girl you are, Angenna. I said you should be schooling your brain to do something with real potential for a better way of life AND he was taking advantage of your capabilities."

"What did he say?"

"Amazingly enough, he agreed he should never have allowed you to stay at home, but then he followed it up with 'Din'a fret, woman, she'll get there in time will our Gen, have no fear." She paused and looked into space. "You see... he could never sell up; the Dales and their tyrannical landscape with life growing on the land are as precious to him as breathing. If he had to live in the town he would split in two … half would still be here."

"But this is about you, Mum, I'm not asking for myself. Do you think he would find help so you could do less?" Genna was hanging in, determined to ignore the smoke screen her mother had thrown up.

Jose's gaze lingered out of the window at the surrounding fields before she answered. "No, Gen, I don't think he will yet and that's the plain truth."

Shortly before leaving for 'The Unicorn' Issy phoned and sounded totally dispirited and said she would not be out later.

"Has John not phone and put you straight about Leonie?"

"Has he heck as like. Well...he phoned - said it was raining and he would be pleased to get back... not a word about the man eater."

"And you didn't ask, I suppose?"

"He'd have probably done a Bill Clinton and fudged what happened - *'I did not have sex with that woman',* even if he did kiss her and give her boobs a tweak."

"Bill Clinton did more than..."

"YES, I know, I know but you get the drift."

"Issy, you imagination is freaking out."

"I CANNOT stop thinking about it."

"I suppose I know that you mean."

"You do? - Who?"

Issy was quick off the mark. "Oh, no, not me, I...er... just understand. Anyway try thinking about 'The Croft' and when we can have another go at the Rose room." Genna changed direction smartly.

"Heavens! Yes, I had almost forgotten. Ring me as soon as you have a couple of hours to spare and we'll do it."

"What'll it be, William, a pint?"

"You betcha life. I though I was dug into that surgery for the night. Did you manage to sort the sheep?"

"Fly did the job in no time and dad put back the wall. I hardly did a thing."

"Enough to catch a graze though?"

As Genna put down the pint William lifted her hand and ran his fingers lightly down the inside of her bare forearm. The lighter skin showed the wide sharply red peppered mark of a new graze. His fingers were adept and precise. A tingle like an electric current slid down her arm, a sensation quite separate from the soreness of the graze as his fingers touched her flesh.

She smiled giving nothing away. "I never actually noticed it until you…"

He gave her a knowing look as her blue eyes regarded him steadily. He lifted the pint and took a thirst quenching drink. Have you sorted your mother?"

"Tried but to no avail."

"What about holiday work for the boys when school's finished for the summer?"

"That's a thought - I'm sure we'll manage. I shouldn't have rattled on about my idle day dreams."

"Genna, your life has to be given a chance too."

"I don't think….Genna trailed off as one of the regulars thrust an empty glass in front of her on the counter. "All right, Sam, another pint? Been a thirsty day ?"

They were beginning to arrive now, the regulars and the 'oft cumdens' as they were known, the latter easy to spot as they gazed around the pub taking in the country atmosphere, the inglenook fireplace with its shining canister filled with new green and copper beech leaves.

Genna noted a critical moment slipping through her fingers. She would never get to know him properly. It would all come to nought, a romance that never had a chance.

She looked up from the pint she was pulling and gave him a half smile, a frustrated look at their inability to continue the conversation. Something in the look produced an answering chord, a shining response from William. Her courage and strength of purpose, not to mention her attractiveness, must have been quite apparent to him.

"How are you getting home with that cranky truck?"

"I haven't cracked that one yet. I cadged a lift here. Maybe dad'll..."

"I can take you if you like. I'm not dashing off anywhere. You may have to drive though." William frowned at his half empty glass of beer.

"Thanks, William, that's great. She turned to Sam with his freshly pulled pint. "There you go, Sam, that should dampen your thirst." She took his money and gave the change from the till while her heart shouted 'YES!' and a chorus of Halleluiahs.

CHAPTER NINETEEN

The busy atmosphere of the pub which normally Genna enjoyed had become oppressive to the point of where she felt stifled. The early summer evening had brought out Joe Public plus whoever he chose to be with and she was hard worked behind the bar.

Pete had been there and had winked at her but his wife was hovering in the background, a fact for which Genna was truly grateful. If he had thoughts of trying his luck again at taking her home he was going to be disappointed.

While she had been occupied William had taken himself off to talk to various people, only occasionally visiting the bar for more drinks.

It was near to closing time when Pete appeared beside her. "I've told the missus you needed a lift, Gen, I saw your dad bring you. You can't walk back in the dark," he chuckled. "Soon as we've cleaned up we'll be on our way."

"Thanks, Pete, but there's no need, I've ..."

"No trouble at all, darlin', anything for you." He cut her off. She had no time to put him right as he turned abruptly on his heel and disappeared into the back of the pub.

Genna groaned with inward dismay. Obviously Pete had not been aware William was involved. He had not seen him speak to her for any length of time at the bar. She hoped he was not going to make a big thing of it, nothing would be more embarrassing.

The customers eventually thinned out and Pete called last orders from the other end of the bar counter. Genna moved purposefully towards him. "Pete, thanks for the offer but William says he will take me home"

Pete did not look up from where he was stacking bottle. "Don't worry about William, I'll soon put him straight."

"Look, Pete, I don't..."

"My staff are my responsibility, love, I don't need any help." He turned his back on her and moved away.

Genna screamed inwardly and hurried to finish the necessary clearing up. The man was boiling up for something stupid and she must avoid it at all costs. In the next few minutes she caught Williams eye and signalled she would be outside in two minutes. Finishing up she grabbed her purse and made for the door through the back. William was already on the car park waiting for her. It was going to be okay. She glanced back to see Pete following her out, his big bulky frame almost filling the doorway.

"Ah, William, no need to worry about transport for Genna, I've sorted it." He called waving the Range Rover keys.

William frowned. "I don't have to if you..." he murmured to Genna.

"*You do!*" Genna hissed in desperation.

William seemed to get the message. "We

arranged it earlier, thanks, Pete." William called taking her arm.

Pete came striding over to them and shoved William's arm roughly away from Genna. "You've got your own bird , Doc, bugger off!" He growled, his body language held the menace of an all in wrestler about to flatten his opponent.

Genna's heart beat galloped down a race track and would have beaten anything in the derby. She could not believe what was happening and what came next was so quick she hardly saw how it came about.

"That's my business, and you have a wife." She heard William say in even tones.

What he did was more important. Pete's aggressive arm disappeared behind his back as William twisted it sharply, pulling it behind his neck at the same time shoving a foot against the back of the man's knees. The effect, helped by the tilt of the car park, was to drive Pete towards the back door of the pub before he even knew what bolt from the skies had hit him.

"Get in, Gen." William told her.

Genna did, as fast as reality would allow. William was beside her and driving out of the car park all in one breath. The whole thing was over in what seemed like seconds.

"I feel like something happened and I almost missed it." Genna took in a long breath and let it out slowly as they drove through the village.

"Like the Hong Kong prostitute said when she

had a long queue," he turned to Genna, "You gotta be velly quick.' Not that I've been to Hong Kong," he laughed.

"But you've obviously studied unarmed combat?"

"Yes, when I was a student in Leeds. But tell me something, has Pete...done this before - taken you home, I mean?"

"Yes, when the truck conked the other Saturday."

"And it had connections with John's remark on Sunday about you being plagued by the opposite sex."

"John didn't know who or what, but yes, it did. I was commiserating with him about his own experiences. You don't forget much, do you?"

"I was curious but I get the drift. I'll ask no more."

After the beery stuffiness of the pub William suggested they stop at the top of the moor and get a breath of fresh sir. Standing next to each other beside William's estate car they looked out over the moonlit moor and breathed in the green, cool smell of the night air.

"I guess this business with Debora must have left you a bit spaced out."

"In some ways it was my fault, the physical attraction blotted out things I failed miserably to take heed of. She was actually very keen to get engaged. I was carried along when I should have put on the breaks. I really did not know her that well...not as well as I know you in fact."

"Do you know me well?"

"Oh, daft things, like how you throw you cake

around when you come out for tea.."

"William! You horror!"

"Well I'd rather talk about you than Debora." He smiled, resting a casual arm round her shoulders.

"Sometimes it does things good to air them."

"I haven't noticed you taking that advice," he turned his head to look at her.

"I suppose it's like Issy said, when something can be done to put things right, like your treatment of mother's condition, it makes sense but if the problems are too big nothing is going to make them go away, however much you talk."

"Is that how you see the farming set up?"

"Not just us, so many farmers. There's no alternative but to just get on with it as best you can."

"It sounds like we're a couple of 'no hopers', doesn't it?"

Genna could hear the smile in his voice as he gently squeezed her shoulders. She snuggled up to him, her head under his chin, making herself available as she intended.

It was all it took. He turned her to face him and hands on her shoulders, kissed her, gently at first. As he realised her response was wholehearted he increased his efforts until she was engulfed in his arms, overwhelmed and almost scared by her feelings of love and desire.

"Genna? He pulled slightly away and looked t her enquiringly but there was no way she wanted to stop.

"I think we'd be more comfy in there." She told him nodding towards the car.

William let his fingers disappear into her dark hair as he held her head, nuzzled her ears and kissed her mouth so sensually it made her dizzy. After some moments she took his hand and led him towards the estate car.

The moon became elusive, playing games behind the clouds, casting ghostly moving shadows across the dark moorland outside the car but the activities of the lovers in the back eventually steamed up the windows and they were not aware of the shadows.

Genna moved to sit up as they lay on the rug in the back of the estate car. Her hair brushed his shoulder and he moved his hand lovingly over the contours of her body, revelling in the smooth texture of her skin.

"What's the matter?"

"I've lost my knickers!"

"That's not fatal."

"No, but what if somebody found them in the back and...?

"I'd tell them I'd had an emergency. Shut up and come here."

Genna could hear the smile again in William's voice and lay back to luxuriate in the feel of his long legs entwined with hers and his body taking over her own once more.

DIARY NOTES.

January, 1945.

I have been given compassionate leave. I said my mother was ill; in fact I know she was distraught. SOMETHING TERRIBLE HAS HAPPENED. I can hardly write it down. She told me Gee was worse after I left, more remote and staying in the hideaway for longer spells, gazing into space. I know he always felt secure there, nobody would be able to find him. She would close the panelling door every night and open it for him the next morning - then, Oh, god! One morning there was the most awful smell of gas when she opened the door. He had left the fire on unlit.

I was extraordinary that we should have a gas supply in the house or even in the village, something to do with being near kettlington, probably father's influence and his money when he was ill. I will curse gas for the rest of my life.

Gee could have done it on purpose, although he never actually spoke of taking his own life. We will never find out. He used to make up the day bed and sleep on it and he looked so peaceful as though he were just asleep but his life was there no more.

Mother gave me a large brandy and said we must sit down quietly and decide what must be done. After I had seen him I was too shocked to think.

I told mother we must notify the Authorities but she would have none of it. She said we would be in trouble for harbouring a deserter and there would be an awful palaver over the suicide. We could even be suspected of murder and our names would be dragged through the papers. The village would be in an uproar. I could see she was right.

I said we should at least tell his mother. We have the address but she insisted it would be the same outcome should his father find out. Better his mother should think Gee was still alive and his father that he was missing.

The desperation of those moments was too terrible, my misery knew no bounds. At least when I had Gee I had somebody to care for, now there would be only mother. But she had stood by me and I must do the same for her. Her strength as ever, was rock solid and I would never have been able to carry out what we had to do without her. I cannot bear even to think about it let alone write it down. I will have to wait until I have found some sort of equilibrium, if I ever do.

Lying in bed listening to the night sounds through the open window, Genna was half awake and half asleep pondering over and over on the wisdom of telling Issy about her liaison with William. Issy was her one and only closest friend and, of course, Genna knew she would be all for their togetherness. Her opinion about what to do, or how she could best approach the situation would be invaluable. There was that one big BUT - would she keep her mouth shut?

She knew Issy's enthusiasm was a force to be reckoned with and not something held in bounds by a sense of confidentiality. She would probably arrive at bursting point and tell William how overjoyed she was, then ask him when the wedding was likely to be. It would be a total embarrassment to William and the last thing ever Genna wanted.

Had Issy phoned, Genna knew she could have fallen into the trap and told all but Issy was in one of her tragic states since seeing John depart with Leonie and no amount of reassurance would work. Genna recognised the pattern from past experience. This time, being low in confidence, uncertain about John, pot and all, she was unable to think of much else. The cat on the hot tin roof' syndrome would probably continue until John returned and straightened everything out, hopefully having kept his celibacy in one piece.

Genna felt her lift home with William had been an emotional watershed. She realised how all her pent up feelings had been given full rein. William had been a supremely kind and considerate lover. Under his educated hands she had suffered no pain from the experience. It had been passionate, a far more earth moving trip than she ever imagined, taking her to a different land. He certainly knew how to work the magic.

Although he had not mentioned love there was no way Genna could think of
that he had abused the privilege she had bestowed of giving up her virginity. He had taken care to make it memorable for her; not only that they had giggled and enjoyed each other with the

glee of small children finding some new exciting game.

The following day a large bouquet had arrived at the farm - a mass or irises, big white daisies, yellow carnations, freesia and something peach Genna did not know the name of. 'Don't ever buy a car' the caption read and was signed W.XX.

Genna smiled happily, walking on a cloud, the euphoria of the Wednesday experience still with her. However, as time wore on the phone call she had hoped for did not materialise. There was no way she could ring William at the surgery and she did not know his personal number for being on call, to thank him for the flowers. Ringing 'The Rectory and asking for William could have really set things alight if Issy answered.

He had said nothing about love - well, could he, so soon after the Debora debacle? Could it have been just casual sex on his part? The elation she had felt began to melt and leave her with misgivings as to whether she had taken the right course.

She was just leaving the minibus at the garage after depositing the children on Friday afternoon when, back in the village she spotted John's blue merc pulling up outside the estate agents. She must see him and apologise for breaking his confidence hoping to do some good by telling Issy about Leonie.

"Don't worry, Genna, I'm glad you did," he told

her still sitting in the car as she spoke to him through the open window. "That was only the start of things. The whole situation is quite out of hand."

"Dare you tell me?"

"Tell you! I need your help and I don't really want to meet Leonie. Are you going home now?"

"Yes, but I don't know how. Dad dropped me off."

"Great! Get in and I'll drive you back."

Genna climbed in beside him and he told her of his Highland trip while he drove.

It had started on the way up to Stirling when Leonie's delicate little hand had rested on his thigh while she as pointing out something. John had smiled and removed it.

When they arrived at her house in a shady tree lined street, Leonie had insisted he had a 'wee break' before going on - a nice cup of tea before her mother came back because her mother was dying to meet John.

"I told her - 'love to, Leonie but I have a long way to go yet'. Then before I could grab a breath an arm snaked around my neck and all that torso and legs draped itself around me. I was drowning, Genna, fast.

Genna suppressed a smile, and waited for him to go on.

"Next thing her mouth had latched on to mine and her tongue was cleaning my teeth." John rolled his eyes. "She was really press up against me in the car, then she started 'Oh Johning' and wiggling. You may not believe this, Genna, but I was too worried to actually enjoy it for thinking about how to get out. AND a vision of Issy was looking over me saying how she would never marry a man she couldn't trust. Anyway I prised Leonie off and I think I managed not to hurt her feelings."

"What on earth did you say."

" It was quite reasonable really, I said 'Leonie I cannot do this to you - make this a casual quicky.' I nearly said and then meet your mother but I didn't. 'You deserve more, you're special - not *that* kind of girl. I don't have time now and I am sort of spoken for.' I don't know that Issy will have me yet, do I? Talk about the great escape!"

"That was ingenious, John," Genna replied brightly but there was a nagging dismay starting to eat at her.

"Anyway I bolted out of the car and went to get her bag from the boot. I though she wasn't going to get out but, thank God, she did and then looked at me with tears in her big blue eyes, would you believe, and said it was the nicest thing anyone had ever said to her. I was so wonderful and her mother so wanted to meet me. Needless to say, I was out 'a there whatever her mother would love to do."

Genna ducked her head again to stop the smile showing.

"I'm just not used to this sort of monogamy stuff and Issy's sure to ask what happened. What on earth do I tell her?"

"Well... better than denying anything, tell the truth."

"*WHAT?*"

"Yes, say that you had to fight off Leonie like a tiger to keep your mind and body for her. She'll just love that."

"Oh! Genna that's just genious - wicked. I'm just hoping Leonie's cooled off by the time she get's back. I'm dreading going into the shop."
Incidentally, the tower house I've inherited is such a male preserve, only men and a crusty old house keeper. The sooner I marry Issy and take her up there the better."

Genna got out of the car wondering how Issy would cope with that scenario, while she, herself, tried to come to terms with John's remarks about Leonie being too good for a one night stand. The dread of it descended on her. Could that be how William saw her - a convenient quicky after the pub? She, after all, had been the one to instigate the love making and although it had been marvellous beyond words for her, had it been casual - casual sex, with nothing special about it for him?

God forbid he should think of it like that when her very heart and soul had marched in to give her all. She would have to wait to thank him for the flowers. What would he say: 'I'm afraid you led me astray after a few beers.but it was fun, wasn't it?' All because *SHE WAS THAT SORT OF GIRL*. Pete had tried to pull her, so why not him? She shuddered

in self-disgust as her winged flight to heaven
crashed to earth.

CHAPTER TWENTY.

So often Genna had heard it said that disasters usually came in threes and the following days seemed to bear that fear out, although it had not started that badly.

"What beautiful flowers, Genna. Who are they from?"

"An admirer." Genna smiled sheepishly, keeping her secret. She relented the next minute noting the look of disappointment on her mother's face at being shut out. "Right, Mrs. McFaiden, I'll do a deal with you: if you tell me truthfully why you are so scared of gypsies, I'll tell you who these flowers are from."

"You scheming tyrant!" Her mother came back at her then looked thoughtful and smiled. "Well, I suppose it's not such a terrible thing, I was so ashamed of it when I was little... it has been hard to overcome."

"Go on then." Genna tweaked a long blue iris to stand better at the back of the vase where she had arranged the flowers the previous day.

"I never liked remembering about it, there was such fear involved..." Jose took a deep breath and continued. "As a child I was scared to death the gypsies would come to claim me." She nodded at Genna's raised eyebrows. "Yes, it does sound silly but not to a small child. After I started school a little girl who must have heard me say I was adopted, told me she always wanted to see a gypsy

close to and now she could because she'd heard
her mum say I must have been a gypsy baby."

"A gypsy baby!"

I had long, dark, ever so curly hair and more
colour that I have now. My eyes were blue like
yours. Maybe I did look like a gypsy. The most scary
thing was, this child said I would have to watch out
because the gypsies always came back to claim
their own and I would never escape, they would be
sure to get me in the end."

"Oh! Mum, so you hid every time you saw
Romany caravans?"

"For weeks I was terrified and dared not mention
it to a soul, least of all mother and father. They
were such dears, old to be parents, I suppose, in
their forties. As you know, they died when you
were quite small." I hated talking about being
adopted."

"So did you find out whether there was any truth
in the story?"

"I did eventually ask my parents and told them
why. They laughed but not with a proof positive
answer and, curiously enough, I saw them
exchange quick glances, which made me even
more certain there must be some truth in the tale. I
still hid at the sight of wagons but they never came
for me." Jose smiled "Go on, now it's your turn -
the flowers."

"Oh, the flowers." Genna was casual as though
they were nothing. "They were from William. No
big deal. I did him a favour at the pub...sort of."

"Mmm...I'm not sure I've had the best end of that bargain, Madam!"

"It's all you're getting!" Genna grinned at her and went to clean out the hens.

Issy's telephone call later that day had been a mixture of elation, confusion and disaster. "Gen, there is so much to tell you, I'm tongue tied."

Genna felt she knew quite a bit of it but as Issy set off at a gallop she began to realise it was not all quite what she had anticipated.

"I saw John briefly last night. He called here and couldn't stay long but he did say he missed me dreadfully and he'd tell me all about how he had come to take the man-eater to Stirling - he didn't call her that, of course. We're going out on Saturday for a meal, but Genna, he looked at me so meaningfully and said I must go up to Scotland with him and see the castle - well, it's more like a tower house because he hopes *I'LL REALLY LIKE IT.*"

"Sounds good to me but, Issy, could you slow down a bit. I'm lagging behind."

"What do you think he means? He wants me to like it! Oh, Genna, do you think it means *WHAT I THINK IT COULD?* Issy almost came down the phone along with the words.

Genna smiled to herself at Issy's excitement knowing it was well founded   "Every chance, I would bet."

"Listen though, the other news is really prickly: there's a suspected case of meningitis in the village. It's very hush hush until it's confirmed. The baby was rushed off to hospital earlier today, only ten months old. Father and William are really concerned."

"Issy, how dreadful for the parents." Genna gasped.

Meningitis sometimes comes in small clusters although it's not supposed to be highly infectious or contagious or anything but there would be a bad situation if this turns out to be positive and there are any more cases. Of course that's the worst scenario... anyway they have to wait and see." Issy paused for breath

Genna shivered involuntarily at the thought of the ill baby as Issy returned to her favourite subject - John. The girls concluded by agreeing that if at all possible they would try and visit the Rose room the following morning, Saturday, a good day for police absence perhaps.

DIARY NOTES:
January, 1945.

I think am feeling more able to write this down now. In some strange way it has helped me before to come to terms with things that have happened as when Rory and Tom died, only Gee's death is much worse for me.

The awful business with his body, the body I knew so well , will be something that stays burned into my memory for every. We dressed him carefully

and wrapped him up well in his airforce greatcoat coat as though we were scared he would catch cold. He was quite tall and heavy for the two of us to carry, even though he had lost weight.

We decided it would be unwise to bury him too near the house, it would have to be further away. There is the big rock where Rory once kissed me, we decided that would be the right place.

The grave we dug was probably not deep enough, the ground was very hard. I was sobbing as we threw the earth back over him so I could hardly see where it was going for tears. Mother actually put her arms around me as she led me away and said we must always keep people away from our land; in fact we must keep ourselves to ourselves for quite some time.

I suppose as a resting place he could have asked for nothing better. He may easily have been shot to bits in the skies over Germany like the boys. May be I could have coped better with that.

I will know where to grow flowers in the future, he loved daffodils. Near to the stream in the trees the grass is long and unkempt but he liked the peacefulness of the woods with only the birds to listen to. The memory is so fresh and ghastly in my mind. Mother was right, there is no other way. I don't expect I shall write much after this. It will be over soon, the war, the life I lived, everything.

Genna hung out the washing in the pale sun of Saturday morning, hoping against hope the meningitis crisis had been sorted for William.

She reflected about all that had happened since Issy's return to Elvingdale: the knickers were still grey, that much had not changed but things had hotted up since digging up the body; Issy's accident, the discovery of the Rose room, her mother's illness solved, all had been important milestones, not the least of which had been her overpowering passion for William. Whether he returned her feeling was another matter.

Nevertheless, she felt somehow she had grown and matured in her own esteem. William may not be entirely lost but Issy had found a soul mate in John and may not remain in Elvingdale long. Would everything revert to black and white again?

She finished hanging the clothes and picked up the old wicker basket that looked moth-eaten but wasn't, as she heard her mother's voice from the yard.

"Genna, the news from the village is not good." Jose shut the door of the truck as Genna met her in the yard. "There are two confirmed cases of meningitis. I suppose that poses real problems for the Farringtons."

Her mother's statement pulled Genna up sharply making her heart jump and feel a stab of dismay for the families involved. The only thing to salvage from the situation, she told herself, was the fact it could be the reason William had not contacted her.

"I expect the surgery will be overrun with mothers demanding vaccination of some sort, or with kids who had headaches, upset tummies, anything the least bit suspect," Genna replied.

"Of course they will feel obliged to make sure their child doesn't have it and I understand it is not so easy to diagnose." Jose went on. "Well, that's what the gossips gave out when I went down with the eggs."

"Was the truck okay?"

"It got me there. Your father says it's alright. I'm not sure I believe him."

"It'll get me to Issy's later this morning, I hope."

The truck did just that. Genna parked it at the top of 'The Rectory ' drive by the front door steps so that she could run it forward when she left. There was no sign of William's estate car.

Issy, looking reasonably normal, appeared at the front door with Fifi and they set off up the lane on foot to 'The Croft'. Issy was walking more strongly, even though she had on the light plaster and the help of her father's stick.

The sky was heavy with unspilled rain and it seemed as thought the weather was about to crack wide open after the hot spell.

"I'm afraid the village has the atmosphere of the plague," Issy started.

"You mean the cases of meningitis?"

"There are two so far...but the first little baby has dies, the bacterial form - it's the worst sort. Oh God! Father and William are both pretty shot at. They are keeping things going like clock work on the surface but they cannot afford to miss any new cases."

"It must be devastating for them." Genna could imagine William must be feeling awful, probably trying to pacify a distraught mother. "I hope to heaven there are not anymore."

"It seems so awful there's nothing we can do to help."

"What about John and his grandfather's estate, Will it make him wealthy?" Genna tried a positive tack.

"You mean his inheritance and being a Laird?"

"What else? He's in the land business already and if he runs things efficiently he could end up seriously rich. You may be thrown into the international jet set; skiing at Klosters, the London season - you know Henley Regatta, Ascot, Wimbledon, then up to your place to shoot grouse on the glorious 12th. Oh! And not forgetting the possibility of some nice little hacienda tucked away on the Med. for out of season sunshine; that is of course, if you marry him."

Genna - hold on, I'm supposed to be the one with the wild imagination and where did you find all this high life formula?" Issy stumbled on an uneven bit of drive in her surprise and lent heavily on her father's stick. Genna put out a steadying hand.

"Me - I've a brain full of useless information. I read about things and they stick. I mean it though, Issy you could be in the money with John."

"Mmm... with my luck I'd probably fall in the river

at Henley, if I haven't already hit a tree and broken something skiing. I would like Wimbledon though and the moors in August, not to mention fewer tourists than here. I'm not sure about the being rich bit. John may not have marriage in mind, rich or poor but I would be happy with either." She glanced at Genna who had a faraway look in her eye.

"It's so easy to think money doesn't matter when you've enough to do what you want - not for material things, clothes or possessions, it's not having *time* that means poor to me. Just take mum and dad for instance, they're not rich in the money sense but they are living the way they want to live so in their way they are rich. Do you see what I'm getting at?"

"Sure, I'd be rich with a proposal from John even if he inherited a hovel. I was carried away by his wanting me to like the place in Scotland, it could mean anything. As things stand at the moment, I don't know where I'm going, standing in the middle of King's Cross station as it were, without a ticket. That blasted predator Leonie, WAS hot for his body. When I think about it I could scream. He hinted as much but said he would tell me all about it tonight."

Genna was quiet hoping John got his 'true story' straight but at the same time, sure he wanted nothing less than Issy for his wife. She sensed a distinct foreboding about the house as they approached. All was eerily quiet as they walked slowly up between the tattered flower beds and the abandoned lawns bordering the drive. The ghosts of the past that must drift through the rooms were surely watching them from the high windows.

Fifi, eager for more pigeon sightings, clattered ahead on the bare boards once they were inside. The Rose room presented the same time-warped scene as the panelling swung open like a door into the 1930s and 40s. The smell of agitated dust could not be missed. The two keys sat awaiting them on the gate-leg table by the window.

"What do you bet that small one fits the cupboard over the fireplace?"

Genna carefully tried it in the lock and once more a door swung open revealing the inside of the small cupboard in the middle of the mantelpiece.

"Is there anything inside?" Issy's curiosity bubbled as Genna fished back into the space.

"There is something...I believe it could be the jackpot." Genna felt a tingle surge through her as she pulled out a black hardback book. "It looks a bit like one of those five year diaries but there are no dates, only lined paper ...Oh, wait... there's writing here and there. The light's so bad I can hardly read it. We'll have to open the window."

Genna went to the window and, ignoring the rain which had started, tried giving it a push as Issy picked up the book and peered to read the faded writing.

"This may tell us everything. We must start at

the beginning but where the hell does it start? There's a date here, Summere, 1937." Issy's curiosity and excitement made her impatient.

Genna's efforts to open the window at last paid off and a gust of wind and rain rushed through the gap before she could close it slightly.

"Here... look." Genna joined Issy at the table, flipped back pages and pointed, I saw something nearer the front. It begins 'Visit from Rory and Tom' they must be the cousins Mrs. Clarke talked of."

The girls started eagerly to read the faint words. They were both quite unaware that the panelling door on its silent hinges had swung to after the gust of wind, slowly closing without so much as a click, leaving them securely locked in the Rose room.

CHAPTER TWENTY-ONE

Both Genna and Issy were so engrossed in reading the diary of Emily Gatenby that neither of them paid any attention to the door, or the fact they were trapped in the Rose room.

"This is utterly amazing," Issy gasped at the details the young Emily had written about her life, "That mother sounds a right old buzzard not telling her the facts of life."

"You have to remember, Issy, those facts were never discussed openly, they were taboo in the best of families. It wouldn't be out of the ordinary."

When they came to the part about Emily being kissed by Rory, Genna was quick to recognise the significance of the place "Issy, this is too much of a coincidence, it must be the big rock where we found the body. Perhaps it was a cousin we dug up after all."

Issy had skipped on further. "She's sent to boarding school. She'd learn the facts of life quickly enough there and look at this about her father dying and oh... Genna, she kisses Rory's name on his letter; it's so poignant."

"She did have an odd sort of growing up, isolated and escaping into books," Genna noted. "It mentions Marion, that's Mrs. Clarke. It's hard to imagine her being a young girl."

"Even harder to imagine Emily Gatenby being young if you'd seen her like Wills and I used to when we were little. She used to shout like somebody batty if she found us trespassing in her wood."

Genna read on. "It must be the late 1930s before World War II. The boys are about to join the RAF and there's more about giggling with Marion Clarke. Remember she said Emily was a crazy driver. Her mother thinks that driving an ambulance she'd kill more wounded than she'd save. I like that."

Both girls became subdued as they read the next faded and sad lines about the war and the cousins' deaths in the Battle of Britain. "That takes care of that then." Issy commented, "not Rory."

"It was Genna's turn." Would you believe it! She joined the WAAF. to get her revenge! Mrs. Clarke didn't tell me that."

There was silence in the room as the two read about the war and Emily's life in the WAAF. With its hardships and difficulties. It was not until they came across the account of her meeting George Bigham-Wade that they looked at each other with wide eyes.

"He became her lover! Could it be him?" Issy was jumping fences to get to the winning post.

Genna stopped reading quite taken aback with the words she read. She looked into the middle distance realising this described exactly the feeling she had experience with William. "A flight of emotion to a sun filled heaven," she murmured almost to herself. Not only that but, in the same way as Emily, she could not bear to tell anyone of her love for William in case nothing came of it. She was not unique, here was a woman some sixty years ago who felt exactly the same about her predicament. She looked quickly back to the pages before Issy wondered at her preoccupation but Issy was equally thoughtful.

"I hope nothing happens to Gee, or he fancies another WAAF. She'll go under if he does."

Genna continued reading, putting her own thoughts to the back of her mind but not however, before she had admitted to herself she cared about William equally as much as the girl in the diary cared about her Gee.

It did not take long before the truth of the events became obvious to them, the facts of Gee's crash, his concussion and long spell in hospital, followed eventually by Christmas in the Dales from where he failed to return to his squadron.

"It's got to be him, Gen, got to be!" Issy's excitement grew so that she missed what Genna was holding up.

"Look! Look! Issy, it's a letter from his mother stuck between the pages and it's about the jewellery. It says it could be worth quite a bit. And she's sent him £250."

"That was then, what about now? I expect you could add at least a nought to that, even more" The pair read on until Issy stopped again.

"What's this for November, 1944? She writes he's stayed there for nearly a year and she cannot understand how he doesn't want to be part of the world anymore." Issy's finger traced the sentence." You know what I think - what I said when we were guessing." Issy smiled cynically.

"You mean he was keeping both mother and daughter happy. No, I don't agree. I think he had a bad case of depression but I don't expect we'll find out by the way things are going - look!"

"Oh God! Genna, YOUR RIGHT, January, 1945 - it's all too much...oh no!" Issy almost shrieked in dismay. "He died in this room on this day-bed. Issy pointed a straight finger in that direction. "I've gone cold all over. It must have been terrible for her."

"Poor Emmy! She didn't have much luck with her men." At least, Genna consoled herself, the spectre that had haunted her imagination had now form and substance. Learning about him as a once living human being would help her lay the ghost of her nightmares holding out the key in skeletal fingers.

"I suppose that's the end. At least we have solved the mystery. We can go to the police and say 'ya boo sucks', look how clever we are" Issy sounded disconsolate.

"I feel so sad for her. It's almost as though I knew her. It's such a grim story, the two women burying him tucked up in that coat, just like we found him." Genna flicked the pages idly. Hang on a minute ...it's not the end - there's a gap. I think I saw some more... look, February, 1945." The two craned their necks over the diary.

DIARY NOTES.
February, 1945.

When I returned to my Unit I applied for release on compassionate grounds because of my mother's ill health. The war is nearly over anyway.

That is the story, the fact is I myself am not well. I have felt dizzy and have started to be sick in the early mornings. I thought at first it was anxiety over Gee but then I realised I could be going to have a baby.

I AM ECSTATIC OVER THE THOUGHT OF GEE'S BABY ...but now things are changing. I cannot be discharged yet. They have given me indefinite leave on compassionate grounds on account of mother's illness and nobody to care for her. She took to her bed fooling the doctor quite easily. She is quite well. I dare say normal demob will take care of my condition in the long run but of course, I have to keep very quite about it. It certainly does not show yet. This was all mother's idea. I always knew she could move mountains if she wanted to.

"Great Heaven! She's pregnant!" Issy grinned happily.

"Just imagine, there may be a little Gee wandering around somewhere." Genna murmured, then lifted her head. "Issy, can you hear something?" Issy looked up from where she was eagerly about to turn the page and continue reading. "What?"

"Issy cocked her head on one side listening. "Oh hell, I can. Do you suppose it's from the village, an ambulance with another case of meningitis?"

Genna dropped the diary and went quickly to the window to peer through the rain sodden view. "I can see a flashing blue light in between the trees. It's at 'The Rectory'".

"At our house? Surely they wouldn't bring a meningitis case to..."

"It's Saturday, the surgery maybe..." But Genna got no further.

"Genna! **It's father...I know it's father,**" Issy squeezed out the words, "he's looked so grey and anxious. Wills told him to take it easy. Oh, Genna I HAVE to go...now."

As she spoke there was a howl from the other side of the door as Fifi, having sneaked out in search of more exciting livestock, made her presence felt at being shut out.

"CHRIST! Genna, it's shut," she gasped, we're trapped in! Do you realise... WE CAN'T GET OUT!" Issy shouted the words and Genna knew Issy was about to lose it completely as she thumped uselessly on the wall with her fists. The situation was made worse by Fifi raising the howling decibels and throwing in a load of barks.

Genna looked quickly to the window and back again. There was little hope of climbing out that way, the gap between the central tilted pane was not big enough, even should there be a convenient drain pipe to climb down. Issy was yelling at her wildly and begging her to do something. For a moment she felt panic rising in her chest. She took a deep breath, went over to Issy and grabbed her hand. "Stop, Isso, and sit down." Genna told her firmly. She did not know how she managed to keep her voice calm but she did somehow, at the same time leading Issy to a chair and pushing her into it.

After a few minutes her friends hysteria subsided to a quieter selection of sobbing and heaving. "Look, we've got to think and keep calm. Do you have your mobile?"

"Issy's eyes widened and, for a moment she managed to collect herself but only until she realised the truth. "Genna, it's in my bag at home and anyway it isn't charged. Oh! damn, damn, damn!" She wailed, "isn't that just typical of me. I'm such a disorganised fool."

"Issy, that's just not true. Stop thinking the worst about your father and we ARE going to get out. There is sure to be a way. Nobody could construct this room as a prison from inside."

"It said in the diary that... her mother shut him in at night and let him out first thing in the morning." Issy dragged her hand across her wet face.

Genna felt like Scarlet O'Hara who never had a handkerchief. She put here arm around Issy's shoulder instead. "She probably feared with his state of mind he may want to wander off at night or something daft and she wanted to keep him safe, or feel secure. She was a fair old control freak at the best of times." Genna talked quietly waiting for Issy's sensibility to take over. Issy glanced anxiously towards the window. Genna distracted her sharply.

"Come on... we've got to start hunting for another way to open this door...and then we'll get out of here. OH! for heaven's sake shut up Fifi!"

Rose hunting was not quite the same task inside the room as out of it; no Tudor roses were to be seen. Genna began to look determinedly along the wall were the door opened . The décor was vaguely a grubby Laura Ashley with a dado, the lower half being different from the upper part of the wall; a line of dark woodwork separated the two. Still not a single Tudor rose in sight.

After some minutes of hunting around the walls of the room Genna went back to the door. The ambulance, she noted, had stopped wailing but Issy still looked stressed as she helped her search.

"It's got to be here, just got to be." Genna muttered as she looked along the woodwork. The dim light in the room did not help matters and she bent down to look closely at the wall. It was then she saw something that brought forth a mew of excitement - a join and for no apparent reason.

"Have you found it Gen? Oh, I hope to God you've found it."

"I don't know. Perhaps I can get my fingers under this join." Genna found her fingers were shaking as she tried to prize up the piece of woodwork next to the join. Like the door to the room, it unexpectedly lifted with the greatest of ease and a brick length opening hinged back to reveal a Tudor rose. "It's got to be it, Issy. Quick, where's my purse, I put the key back in it." There was a mad scramble to find Genna's purse from where she took the key with hands by now shaking visibly.

The piece of woodwork having hinged away from the wall, left a clear gap enabling the head of the key to go round the rose and with space to turn it. Genna took a deep breath and tried but it would not turn.

"Oh f...ing hell... it won't turn. The mechanism must be fouled up." Issy watching, was becoming desperate again.

"Shut up, Issy, don't be such a pessimist. It may go the other way. Instead of pulling downwards, Genna tried upwards. The door clicked and swung open to let in a joyful Fifi who bounded at them nearly knocking them over in the process.

"Oh, thank God for that. Gen, you're a marvel, I really had a bad case of claustrophobia. I just prayed and said I'd never be wicked again if only we could get out."

"Come on, grab the diary and let's go." Genna was keen to move.

"Hang on a minute, what are we going to say to the police." Issy's imagination had ground to a halt.

"Piddle easy... nothing until we've read the rest of this. Heaven knows what other stuff Emily's going to come up with." Genna was at the controls.

CHAPTER TWENTY-TWO

By the time they arrived back at 'The Rectory' the girls found the place deserted. Even though they had hurried, progress from 'The Croft' had been hampered due to Issy's leg plaster. Genna dreaded to think the strain being put on the healing tendon.

Issy limped into the house and began to make hasty telephone calls. When she eventually put down the telephone she sighed heavily in resignation. "He's had a heart attack. They've taken him to Kettlington General...I know he doesn't get enough exercise and he loves things like sugar'n eggs and double cream. I bet his arteries are screaming with cholesterol."

As she started to sob, tears coursed down her cheeks and Genna put her arms round her for the second time that day. "Come on, Isso, they can perform miracles these days. He's still alive, isn't he? He needs you to be cheerful when he perks up."

"Yes, yes, you're right, I'll have to go and hold mother together."

"But you can't drive with the pot, you'll have to let me take you." Genna reminded her, at the same time wondering who really would be doing the holding together - William probably.

It was another hour by the time Genna dropped Issy at the hospital and made her way home. The Farrington family would not need her presence at such a time of anxiety. She would have been in the way. Issy had promised to let her know how her father was as soon as she could. Genna would have to wait for that.

Her mother looked up in surprise as she came into the kitchen. "Ah, Genna I thought you must be lost. I have to go out and I need the truck. Is it okay. I imagined it had packed up again.

"Er… no but we were sort of…lost. You'll never believe what happened." Genna barely had time to mention the diary and how they had been locked in the Rose room, except to say that they now thought they knew whose body they had dug up, before her mother was on her way.

"It all sounds very weird. I'll be back in time for you to go to 'The Unicorn' and you can tell me the details then," her mother called over her shoulder, "and your father was out digging up potatoes last time I saw him."

"Mum, don't rush. I'm going to ring Pete and say I have a splitting headache and I just cannot face tonight."

She failed to add the headache had more to do with the fact that Pete had been surly and had hardly spoken when she worked in the pub on Thursday and Friday. Genna realised her position there was becoming impossible and she would have to quit the job, the sooner the better.

The house was quiet except for the steady pitter-patter of rain. Her father had not come in yet and must still be working even though the rain was coming down more heavily. Genna sent up a silent prayer for the life of Harvey Farrington as she made herself a cheese and pickle sandwich and a cup of coffee. She picked up the diary from the table to read it while she ate.

She sat thinking about what a load of stress William must be facing. It seemed of no importance that he had not been able to contact her when there were lives at stake. She knew she ached to see him and soon, to have his arms around her and confirm how it felt when he made love to her.

When she thought about him every small movement he made seemed beautiful, every word he spoke had a special meaning to it. Would it ever happen again? Did he have any special feeling for her. She had no idea and it was no good speculating, or building herself up only to be disappointed. The point was, she could not stop herself being in love with him so that hardly anything else mattered. She turned to the diary in the hope of distraction.

They now had a clear and amazing picture of what had happened to Emily Gatenby's lover but the fact of her being pregnant put a different face on things. Genna started to read the final date under the heading of February, 1945.

The terrible…terrible thing is that mother says I cannot keep the baby - *Gees baby. I cannot bear it. She says it is not because she does not want the* *child, or would not love it, but simply that we could hide a man but not a baby. It would have to be registered so it could have identity papers and milk and orange juice and there would be no answer to the questions about the father or where he came from.*

If anything did come to light - anything at all, we would be back to harbouring a deserter and burying a corpse. There would be the constant threat of being found out and should this happen I would have the stigma of being an unmarried mother and bearing a bastard.

The alternative is to leave the baby with somebody anonymously but who? Besides I do not want to do this at all. I would take all the risks. I want Gee's baby more than anything.

Genna shook her head sadly knowing already how unacceptable illegitimacy used to be especially in a village such as Elvingdale. Geoff Cordingly bringing milk or even the postman would only have to hear a mew of a baby crying and the village would have the news like a swarm of bees with a message of new honey. She continued reading.

May, 1945.

The Germans have surrendered. The wireless is ecstatic and I feel miles from it all. I am fighting the thought of giving away the only thing I have left of Gee. Mother has been so good and has sheltered and looked after me so well. When I talk of the possibility of keeping the child , I can see all her arguments but it would bring so much joy to us, I feel sure. Even so I have to think of her too. Perhaps she will change her mind.

JULY, 1945
Mother has not changed her mind. She says it will be hard at first but we must bear it. I have resigned myself to the fact that I cannot keep Gee's baby. It has been kicking hard against my sides, it must be a boy, and yet I will never see him walking and running through the days of childhood. Life has been so cruel to me. When he's gone I shall be left alone with mother in isolation in this undesirable residence. The war may be over but I think I am going to hate the peace.

Genna felt tears pricking her eyes at the plight of Emily Gatenby. The history book she had read told her that the working class were usually to poor to care about illegitimacy, the aristocracy so rich it did not matter to them but the middle classes had always been totally bigoted when it came to bastards, even ostracising them in the community.

The picture clicked into place of how Emily Gatenby had become a recluse when her mother had died and she had been left with nothing but the grave in the trees. She read the last tragic sentences.

Having the baby was not as bad as I thought, although bad enough. My daughter was born on

25th. August, 1945 and I would not have survived it without mother, I felt so weak afterwards. We had unravelled some light coloured woollens and knitted the wool up into baby clothes. We dressed the child, a lovely dark haired little girl and wrapped her in a clean piece of sheet. We put her in a basket with the locket that Gee gave me round her neck. Our initials are not easy to read so I have no fear she will be traced to us.

Genna felt a tingle at the back of her knees as she read the date of the baby's birth and her eyes darted along the page to learn the rest.

Mother took her up to the Priory at the top of Lang Brow in the early hours. I was helpless and could do nothing to stop her. Mother said she would ring the bell until a light appeared. They are used to poor soles in distress arriving on their doorstep.

Hidden at a discreet distance she waited until she saw someone pick up the basket and discover the baby. Then and only then did she go back to the car and drive off. (She had managed to scrounge a few petrol coupons for emergencies in case she was 'ill' again.)

I am at least confident the nuns will find a home for the child. I have heard before how they helped place foster children. I wanted to go and talk to them in confidence but mother would not hear of that, she said it was too dangerous and this was the best way. Whatever, it is done now, done and over and that's an end to it.

Genna put down the book in disbelief. Her mouth had gone dry. She could not believe what she had seen. It couldn't be... but there is was, 25th. August; that was her mother's birthday and she had a locket from when she was a child, the one Genna used to borrow.

She must be going mad imagining these things... Her mother Emily Gatenby's daughter! She read the last part again, her heart racing. Even the story her mother had told of her parents silence on the subject of her adoption and her silly fears of being abandoned by the gypsies, all seemed to fit. She held her head in her hands fearing she was not quite sane.

There was, she told herself, only a single link missing in the chain of events that could prove conclusively her mother and the abandoned baby were one and the same person and that, of course, was the place from where her mother had been adopted. Maybe her mother had never known that. She would simply have to wait and ask her.

She picked up the diary feeling slightly dizzy and not quite sure what she was going to do next. As she did so something fell out of the back. She looked down to see a newspaper cutting had fallen to the floor. She bent to pick it up. A date on the paper caught her eye - 1946.

In faded ink a column had been marked out.

Genna saw it offered a reward for the return of
jewellery and she felt a shiver go through her as
she recognised the address as being the same as
the letter from Gee's mother.

*'A REWARD OF £500 is offered for the return of
jewellery owned by Lady Bigham -Wade. A leopard
brooch made from jet, gold and diamonds, a car
brooch with diamonds in the window and a golden
snake choker with ruby eyes.'*

These items were listed as the easily identifiable
valuable pieces. Pearls and more items were
mentioned below. Genna knew she had seen them
with her own eyes, nevertheless she could hardly
believe what she read. There total value in today's
money would surely be a considerable. The
Antique Road Show would just love this lot. She
hated to think what the insurance value would be.

The thought assailed her mind that the time-warp
Rose room and all it held had been waiting there
for over half a century for somebody to discover it.
What her parents would say she could not imagine
and as for Issy... At that moment Genna heard the
yard door open and her father appeared in the
kitchen soaking wet, clutching a sack obviously
holding potatoes.

"Put these away for me, would you, Gen, and
while you're on your feet a cuppa would be nice."

Genna took the potatoes and waded straight in.
"Dad, have you any idea about mother's adoption?
She told me the other day that when she was little
she heard she was a gypsy baby and they would

247

snatch her back, which was why she was so scared. She doesn't really believe that now... but was she an abandoned baby?" Genna felt her heart fluttering waiting for his answer.

"What in the world do you want to know that for? Will it make a big difference one way or t'other?"

"Yes, it could." Genna answered as she put the kettle back on the Aga.

"Well, I'm sorry to have to tell you, love, I know she was adopted but little more. She was always ashamed of being scared of gypsies."

Genna made the tea and put it in front of him, realising that was the end of that until her mother arrived back.

"I'll tell you what, Genna, I'm far more concerned about all this rain. We're going to have a busy day tomorrow shifting livestock from the lower grazing if it goes on. That stream is a right little river now. Never seen so much come down in one go."

Genna's thoughts were buzzing and out of control. She was only half listening to what her father said. She wondered if 'The Rectory' drive would be awash with the stream and how Issy was coping. She should tell her father about Harvey Farrington. She realised at that moment there was one other thing she had forgotten - her mother's silver locket. What had Emily said, the initials were difficult to read, but surely she could...? "In fact, Genna, if you're not doing much in the morning..."

But Genna did not hear, she belted out of the

kitchen and up the stairs making for her parents bedroom. Her mother kept a small box in one of the top drawers of her dressing table. It contained a few precious bits of jewellery and, unless she was wearing it, the locket would be there.

She scrambled through the small drawers and found the box. She quickly opening it and she poked her fingers around to find the locket which should have been easy to see. Nothing. She tried to remember if her mother was wearing it and came to the conclusion she had not noticed it round her neck when she went out. Surely it must be somewhere... then she remembered she had put it on herself when she was trying to look nice in case William came into the pub.

She belted to her own room to look in the place where it would be on top of her chest of drawers - an old china dish with a lid. She lifted the lid and there was the locket.

She picked it up feverishly and gazed at the round scrolled initials. Could they be EG. Combined with GBW, George Bigham -Wade? She was sure they could but not absolutely certain. She ran her thumb over it and realised that of course, it opened. She prized at the notch with her nail and the small lid lifted up. Inside was a curl of dark brown hair. A shiver went through her. Somehow it did not look like her mother's

Could it belong to George Bigham-Wade? If it did, a DNA test may be able to prove it came from the remains they had dug up.

At that moment she heard the truck arrived back in the yard. She turned and galloped out of her bedroom nearly slipping and almost falling on the sloping stretch of floor down the passage.

She stamped down the stairs hardly noticing her father sitting open mouthed at her behaviour. Her mother was just walking through the door carrying various pieces of shopping.

Before she could say anything her father beat her to it. "I think our Genna's losing her marbles. She shot out of the kitchen as I'm telling her something and she's been charging round the house like an elephant on the rampage, not to mention asking daft questions about your parentage. Have you any sedatives, Jose?"

Genna rushed over to her mother, who stepped back to look at her. "Mum, where...where did you come from?"

"Come from?" Her mother was bemused and almost snapped back at her. She glanced warily across at her husband, obviously concerned that maybe he had been serious about Genna's mental state. He shook his head and raised bemused eyebrows in reply.

"I mean it, Mum, from where did your parents adopt you?" She said each word distinctly and crisply as though talking to a child. Her tone communicated the urgency of what she wanted to know.

Jose paused before answering and her reply was rather stiff and formal at being spoken to in such a manner. "I don't know exactly how I came to be an abandoned baby and it appeared that neither did they... maybe it was gypsies," she paused, "I was collected from the care of the nuns at Lang Brow Priory and they thought I had been born on or near the day of 25th. August, 1945."

Genna gave along sigh and collapsed at the table and closed her eyes, her hands holding her head. I t was all true, her mother was Emily Gatenby's daughter, which meant that she was Emily's granddaughter.

CHAPTER TWENTY-THREE

The rain over night had dwindled and Sunday looked a brighter day. If the weather dried up a bit there would be no need to start moving stock from the lower ground as the water levels receded.

Issy had phoned with the news that although not yet completely out of danger her father's condition was stable and they were hopeful for his recovery.

"What about the meningitis?" Genna had asked, which was a genuine enough question but hiding another which was about William.

"There's a third scare but it hasn't been confirmed and the second case is responding well to antibiotics, so Wills is hopeful there will not be any more. Poor old thing, he looks whacked coping with mothers galore, scared to death their offsprings are going to be next, even when it's only a headache. But, Genna, I cannot wait to hear about the diary. Have you read it yet? Was there much more?"

"Yes, I have read it - not a lot more but it was just so incredible... you're not going to believe... look I can't tell you over the 'phone, it is pretty complicated. We'll meet and, hang on to you hat, we have to arrange to contact the police... we'll have to go together."

"GENNA! You WROTTEN THING! No... I don't really mean that, you were brilliant when we were stuck in the Rose room and I lost it but can't you give me a clue?"

Genna refused to budge and instead asked about John.

"Well it just so happens there's a hell of a tale to be told about that but it will have to wait until I see you...so there! I'll give you a hint thought. I'm really, really happy at the way things are going."

Genna had a feeling she knew quite a lot already of the details of John's trip to Scotland but she would only be too pleased to hear the outcome from Issy when they arranged to meet.

The shock waves were at their height when she handed the diary over to her mother to read. After initial disbelief Jose had listened and read as Genna pointed out crucial parts of the faded writing. She looked more and more incredulous when they came to the details of the suicide. She felt her mother fingers tighten as they read about Emily's pregnancy. But it was when her mother read the part where the baby had been left at the Priory that realisation began to dawn how the information about her origins was very relevant and her face mirrored the same amazement and shock that Genna's had done earlier. By the time they had finished Jose had tears running down her cheeks at the plight of the person who had proved to be her mother.

"It all fits...every single bit, like a jigsaw puzzle. Oh... Genna, I just cannot believe it! How did you find this?"

"Issy and I visited the Rose room a few times. It is

understandable how they missed it when the house was cleared. Issy is the one to thank as much as anybody for the discovery if anything comes of it. But we have actually seen the jewellery, it was hidden in the bureau. We joked about the diamonds, we thought the stuff looked nothing at all but from the newspaper cutting it could be a different story when it's all buffed up a bit."

Her mother sat shaking her head, dazed."The truth of the matter is, Genna, I don't think my parents were all that sure if it was official - the adoption I mean. There were lots of things not quite official in the aftermath of the war. Mother was the district nurse and father the postman and they were older but desperate for a baby. They undoubtedly knew the Sisters at Lang Brow. I believe that's why they never said much about what actually happened.

"That does not make any difference to whoever your biological parents were though, does it?"

Her mother could do nothing but agree but then added. "I suppose you'll have to go and give an account of yourselves to the police now."

Genna nodded but could not avoid the finger of apprehension creeping up her spine.

A telephone call to Pete early Saturday found him out so Genna left a message and some time later he phoned back. To her surprise he apologised for making a complete fool of himself.

"Genna, I've done some serious thinking. I was knocked silly after I drove you home. I just went on a massive ego trip. There's no fool like an old fool they say. Will you apologise to William for me? I haven't set eyes on him since - been busy with this meningitis scare, I suppose."

Genna had taken her share of the blame but reminded him he was not that old and he ought to be more careful who he was kissing goodnight.

He asked her most politely if she would continue to work and assured her there would be no more nonsense. She could see no way to refuse his request; after all she did like helping in the pub, it was the only chance she had to meet new people. No matter what became of William, or the business with the diary, it was still a safeguard to earn some money.

She came off the 'phone glad Pete had turned out to have the depth of character to say what he had and like him better for it.

It was Monday morning when Genna met Issy at Bessie's tearoom and they settled down to catch up with each other's news before handing the diary over to the police. There was no sign of Bessie and one of her many helpers brought their coffee.

"Now then, let's have it, this amazing stuff at the end of the diary."

"Genna kept her face straight. " Well, it appears I'm Emily Gatenby's granddaughter." she replied quite casually.

"O...kay...very funny, joke over, now let's have the proper tale."

"It's true, Issy, no joke... all true. Mother was the baby born to Emily and abandoned at the Priory at Lang Brow because her mother couldn't face the scandal and trying to keep it a secret would have been impossible." Genna waved the diary triumphantly. "IT'S ALL HERE!" Her pretence at solemnity became impossible and she had tears in her eyes as she found she was beaming at Issy.

"MY GOD! You're NOT joking! Let's have a look."

"Be careful with it. We don't want to destroy the evidence." Genna was aglow as she gave Issy the diary. "Mother confirmed it and everything fits. It's all quite quite mad and I cannot really believe any of it."

Issy read the details including the newspaper cuttings, with the accompaniment of a lot of oohs and ahhs. "You sound so cool about it. Do you realise, you idiot, YOU could be seriously rich, the jewellery, the house, the whole bloody works, money to burn! Marvellous, Genna."

Genna had scarcely dared to think about the implications of Emily's wealth, whether great or small. It would be building where nothing may exist. Her reply was wary. I don't know about that, there's a long way to go. Maybe mother could inherit something. I can't cross that bridge, Issy. Now come on tell me about you and John. We don't have much time before we have to be on parade."

Issy put down her cup and sighed." She did invite him in, y'know, the man-eater, He said she really was after his body. What DO you think he told me then?"

Genna had a fair idea but kept mum on the subject.

Issy giggled happily. "I fought her off with unbelievable ferocity and managed to keep myself ALL for you, Issy." Issy gesticulated theatrically, "then he said he really was not involved with Leonie but he was silly about me. I reminded him we would have miles of England and most of undulating Scotland between us."

Genna noted her coaching of John had been quite well carried out. "So was that it?" She had hoped for more.

"Oh, we're coming to the best bit now. He said it wouldn't be like that, not if I went to Scotland with him. I could wear a kilt or what the hell I liked as the lady of the local laird."

"You mean..." Genna feigned a thoughtful look, "he was proposing?"

"He nearly ruined it though - said they were a straight laced lot up there, we would HAVE to be married. He sounded apologetic. There wasn't going to be much time before he took up residence and it was a bit remote. If I didn't want to commit myself he wouldn't blame me. I almost shouted at him - marrying me is more for their benefit than mine then?"

Genna groaned inwardly at John's clumsiness but Issy, it seemed, had not intended the moment to slip by. "I reminded him there was someone else he would have to consider."

"Yes, who?" Genna wondered who on earth she had forgotten.

"There's Fifi. I have to think of her future. John rolled his eyes to heaven like a mad thing and called her 'that trouble maker'. I suppose he meant luring me down a mine shaft. I said to shut up she may hear. What do you think he did?"

"I haven't the foggiest." Genna just prayed he got it right.

"He bent down to Fifi my feet muttering 'I'll soon fix her'. I wondered what the devil he was going to do." Issy scowled. "He tapped her on the nose and she sat up and stuck out her white chest beautifully. He then said, 'Miss Fifi Farrington would you do me the honour, along with your mistress, of giving me your paw in marriage.' He lifted her paw and Fifi looked at him disdainfully down her nose, she was so embarrassed. She sneezed with a great nod of her head and he said 'There you are' - all fixed. What about you?'"

Genna chortled with laughter, if John didn't get it just right with Issy he had certainly managed it through her dog which was just as good.

"I told him he was a lunatic, but if push came to shove I'd go along with the team." She paused for breath. "I did say I wouldn't expect her to sleep in our room, she farts and snores all night, although sometimes she does get awfully lonely and I have to..."

"ISSY! You did not say that?"

"Well I did but I couldn't keep my face straight any longer." As Issy spoke more urgently the words came tumbling out falling over each other. "I just peeled with laughter I was so happy. John could only think of one way to stop me and that went on and on for ages, it was scorching kiss, the back slab nearly melted." Issy stopped suddenly and grabbed Genna's arm as her eyes filled with tears. "Oh, Genna I felt so mean and guilty," she sobbed.

Genna's helpless amusement at Issy's dotty nature came to an abrupt halt. "Issy, what on earth…?" She started.

"That I should be so happy when dad's lying half dead in hospital and mother's like a picture of Dorian Grey with anxiety. I feel SO SELFISH!"

Genna took a deep breath. "We all have our own fates to work out, Issy, and they would want you to be happy, I'm sure of that. I'm really glad it worked out for you , so they must be doubly so."

"God! You're right. I'm just wound up about it all."

Genna wished and wished her love life could be as simple. But it would be no time to tell Issy about that.

The interview with the police became reality. The sparsely furnished room was cold and threatening and Genna felt as though she was about to be interrogated but, as she told herself later, it was more to do with her own state of mind than the police's intention.

The questions were endless and Issy told a convincing tale about how they had found the key to 'The Croft' when they were looking for her dog, Fifi, and had forgotten all about it until Saturday when they had discovered how it fitted the back door of the house. Hadn't they gone out of sheer curiosity, as you would, and come across the diary sitting on the table in the Rose room, all quite by chance.

Genna cringed a bit at the edited version of what had happened as it tripped of Issy's tongue, but the police seemed more concerned about the value of the information provided in finding the identity of the body.

Genna confirmed that, yes, they had opened the bureau, the key was in the lock, and there was this grubby pouch full of old jewellery which having read the diary, they realised could be valuable, so of course they had notified the police as quickly as possible.. They were a pair of little white hens who had done no wrong!

When it came to relating her mother's position in the story, the responding body language, as Genna saw it, was definitely sceptical and they were told gravely this would have to be checked out with the necessary parties and they would be notified of the outcome.

One outside in the fresh air Genna heaved a deep breath and Issy, hanging on to her arm for support, shook with silent laughter. Do you think they swallowed the bends in the truth?"

"I'm not sure, I had the feeling we were going to be arrested at any moment for breaking and entering, handcuffs an all."

"Of course not, we solved their potential murder for them, so they should be grateful."

"Well grateful or not, we've done it now, made it official. We'll just have to await the outcome." Genna was realistic.

Returning to the farm, Genna related the news to her mother. Together they pored over the initials on the locket which were still not conclusive evidence as far as they could see. Her mother came to the same conclusion as Genna, it was not use speculating, they would just have to wait.

She went to bed that night with a quiet sense of excitement at the prospect of a great change in her life, although she was not at all sure what it was going to be. However, at the same time it was mixed with despondency at how William may regard their night of passion; it hadn't even been that, just a couple of hours on the moor top in his car, a poor recommendation for a proper love affair. She went to sleep with an aching heart, the despondency winning.

CHAPTER TWENTY-FOUR

It seemed to Genna that life took on a strange dreamlike quality. The following days were a daze of contacting solicitors and a further interview for her mother and herself with the police.

`The next development was the press. Facts were released about the diary and the identity of the body. For the locals it was an astonishing event and the village buzzed with excitement at the return of the news hounds and media. To avoid them Genna played cat and mouse games. She would keep away from the road entrance to the farm and cycle on the old bike round the back of the village. It was an arduous trip but peaceful.

When they discovered her at the pub things were not so easy. Pete stepped in manfully and told them to f**** off and worse. She intended to say nothing about the likelihood of her family connections to 'The Croft' until she had proof positive.

The legal wheels turned surprisingly quickly, no doubt due to the fact that solicitors for the treasury had been advertising for relatives of Emily Gatenby for some time to discover whether the Crown could claim the estate or not.

It was a matter for the law to establish the fact that Mrs. Jose Mcfaiden would inherit the property known as 'The Croft'. For the purpose of selling newspapers, the press had already taken it for granted. Issy did not mind at all and at last Genna had to give way.

"Just one more picture, girls, - you and your friend ...here - hold this, look as though you've just discovered something." A more enterprising picture merchant thrust a book into Issy's hand and backed off to capture the two in frame against the backdrop of 'The Croft' where they had agreed to go to be photographed.

Issy gave them a cheesy smile while Genna appeared less happy and fixed the pack with an icy look as the cameras clicked and flashed once more. Having congratulated herself on avoiding the press so well up until then, Genna cursed silently at stupidly letting Issy talk her into this, saying that once they had what they wanted they would go away. She hoped Issy knew what she was talking about. The local dailies had already told the area how the 'LOST LIFE OF RECLUSE REVEALS MYSTERY OF BODY'

"If this is the sort of thing Royalty have to put up with no wonder they can look fed up at times." Genna murmured to the smiling Issy.

"Okay, Gen, my leg's going to collapse. Help me back into the transport and we'll tell them goodbye for ever." Issy waved her stick and proceeded to go. Genna knew as far as Issy was concerned it had all proved to be blissful light relief from the boredom of the enforced leisure.

For Genna it was shortly after that a further development took place. The ripples from the Emily Gatenby pool were beginning to spread.

The family of the late Sir Anthony and Lady Bigham-Wade had been discovered and, as the dairy told them, George had a younger sister. Through their family solicitors more extraordinary information came to light.

Genna and her mother were invited to the Leeds office of a large London firm of solicitors and found themselves seated on one side of an imposing desk with a dark suited and very formal senior partner sitting opposite to them.

Introductions had to be properly completed. Mr. L. Winters ordered coffee from his silent footed secretary and once they were all settled he spoke.

"Mrs. Mcfaiden, this is quite an extraordinary case. I have to tell you first of all, we have been able to verify the facts of your origins with the Sisters as Lang Brow Priory. Their records show details of the baby left with them on the night of 25th. August, 1945, or the early hours of 26th. We are now satisfied you are that same person by virtue of the fact they placed the infant with local people whom they have named as your adoptive parents."

"Ahh..." Jose breathed a small sound. She did not look at Genna who was sitting quite still as though if she moved it would all disappear or go wrong.

"This, of course, with the evidence you have produced, established Emily Gatenby and George Bigham-Wade as your natural mother and father." The solicitor paused for this to sink in before continuing in even more serious tones. "There are one or two important facts of which I must make you aware with regard to George Bigham-Wade's family. He looked up to convey the gravity of the situation and then continued.

"Sir Anthony, George's father, died sometime after the end of the war but his mother, Lady Bigham-Wade, was younger and did not pass away until the 1960s. It appears she left a codicil in her Will concerning jewellery she had gifted to her son before he disappeared. She hoped, I understand, that Gee, as she called him, would contact her. An advertisement had been placed in the newspapers offering a reward for the return of her jewellery, as you have already seen."

"After the death of her husband she decided to add to this money and advertised again, always convinced that through it he would contact her, or at least she would learn what had happened to her son, George. He would read the papers and make contact, or somebody would recognise the description of the jewellery and do the same. By the time she died it had accumulated to five thousand pounds and this she had asked to be invested in a trust to benefit any of his issue who may know of the whereabouts of the jewellery." Mr. Winter regarded the silent two profoundly once more to see if they were taking in the significant of his pronouncements.

"Should it be no blood relation, then the original reward would be paid out. If, however, it should be a blood relative and Gee already deceased, they would inherit the trust and the jewellery. This condition would apply to and include his grandchildren; otherwise the trust would be returned to his sister or her children.." Mr. Winter paused once more and regarded mother and daughter before him."

"The facts I have to give you about George's sister are really very favourable to your case. She is alive and well but has remained childless - never married after she inherited the family house and fortunes of the Bigham-Wades. She is an academic and travels a great deal with enough money to do whatever she wants. There is no great likelihood of her contesting any serious claim to her brother inheritance." Mr. Winters gave the first sign he was human and smiled at them kindly across the expanse of desk.

Genna had sat listening to him speak as though the situation involved someone quite different and had nothing to do with her. He obviously expected her to question his statement and she frowned trying to align the fact it was herself and her mother to whom he had referred.

"You are saying that having made the find, I will inherit the jewellery and the five thousand pounds?"

The smile remained. Mr. Winter was obviously pleased to be able to impart good news to such a pleasant looking young woman who, although she did not appear to be impoverished, was certainly not a member of the affluent society. She did not look the giddy sort at nineteen, and to give her credit she did not appear to be grasping, or excitable, rather a cool customer in fact.

"I have to tell you, Miss McFaiden, that the money invested in the sixties has done extremely well and there is now considerably more that five thousand pounds involved. The way Lady Bigham-Wade approached it has provided substantial growth, which is what I believe she intended. There is now a sum involved somewhere well over a hundred thousand pounds. What is more, "he continued, the way the trust has been set up you may be able to avoid what would have amounted to a lot of tax AND you will also have the jewellery, which itself is worth a small fortune."

Had she been the swooning type Genna knew she would have slipped quietly to the floor but she was far too strong for that. Mr. Winter was telling them more.

"You are, of course not yet of age, twenty-one that is; this comes into the Will."

Genna nodded, mesmerised by the man's intense look.

"Although you may not have the total sum, you will be allowed to use money from it at the discretion of your parents, or guardians. Had your mother found the jewellery, she would have had full access to the money as she wished but, of course she, as her daughter, already benefits in that she inherits Emily Gatenby's house, land, and investments which will amount to a very comfortable amount..

Genna felt quite unreal as she stepped out into the city sunlight once more. Mother and daughter said little about what they had just been told.

"Shall we find a cup of tea, Genna, I never touched that coffee."

"It's about the only thing I'm capable of." Genna replied, smiling weakly. I cannot really take it in, Mum, all our troubles seem to be over."

Her mother nodded with a look that spoke greater than anything she could manage to say.

The pair sat over a cup of tea in a small student café not far from the solicitors office in Leeds. "This is going to change our lives, isn't it?"

Jose nodded. "I don't think we'll move from Elvingdale. Your father mentioned selling the farm and turning 'The Croft' into a country house bed and breakfast during the summer season, if anything came of this inheritance business. I suppose there are quite a few bedrooms and I would quite enjoy that."

"You could employ some help and garden gently instead of having to slog away all the time with vegetables."

"We could keep some poultry, there are some outbuildings, maybe hens and geese and sell most of our farm land...just keep an acre or two for a few sheep if he wanted,"

"You wouldn't need me, would you?"

"I wouldn't want to lose you, but no, we wouldn't

need you to help in the same way, Gen. It would be so much easier. You could do whatever you wanted with the money Mr. Winters spoke about."

Genna wondered if her mother realised what the words meant to her. She felt like a bird being released into the sky. Her cage had been full of love and security but the wide blue horizon was now open to her. She could try for further education, go abroad, even buy new underwear - no more grey knickers, things she never thought would happen. Her mind could hardly believe the facts but her heart lifted to the ceiling.

Only one thing had not happened as she had hoped. In all the excitement it had been at the back of her mind from where she had tried to suppress it even further. William. Would he ever be part of her life? Now she could have all the things any normal girl would want, would one more be too much to ask?

Emily Gatenby had found very little lasting happiness. She realised she was like her grandmother, not in just her looks but in so many ways. The fondness she had for books and the yearning to read, her inclination to stay on the edge of things rather than be in the middle of them, not to mention her single mindedness in her love affair. Could it be that she, like her grandmother, was not destined to find that sort of happiness?

CHAPTER TWENTY-FIVE

Early summer's green lushness in Elvingdale's old village square had turned the trees to cool canopies of shade, a place where the usual influx of visitors could rest their feet, write their postcards, eat their ice creams, or languish, doing nothing at their will.

Saturdays were usually busy and now with the recent news of 'The Croft' and the identity of the body being revealed with everything but a fanfare of trumpets in the press, the brief meningitis scare had been forgotten.

Anyone who had anything to sell was bent on selling it to the utmost of their ability while the rush lasted. The phone in the McFaiden's farm had been more demanding than for a long time. That particular Saturday the first caller had been Issy.

"How did the legal thing go, Gen?" Issy's voice sounded to be overflowing with energy.

"Simply amazing. Really I have a lot to thank you for in how it happened and we found the diary. I had this feeling you should have been there and taken some credit."

"No way. It's you family's inheritance from your grandparents. Old Emily Gatenby would be in her seventh heaven if she knew." Issy sounded calmer than she had of late.

"It's quite a story. Lady Bigham-wade put the reward money into a trust after topping it up after her husband's death in the hope of finding out what happened to George, or even if he may still be alive. You wouldn't believe how much it's worth now - thousands and if the person finding the jewellery is a relative, they get the reward trust and the jewellery.

"GENNA! You mean you're going to be seriously rich?"

"Not seriously but very adequately in comparison to what we've had before. I feel quite dazed, Issy. Everything seems to be up in the air. There are choices, something I've never had. I suppose I haven't accepted it's all quite true."

"Mmm... You'll accept it when you have money to spend."

"My parents are talking of running 'The Croft' as a country house bed and breakfast in the summer months, you know, home produce a speciality. They would make the garden look lovely again. There's quite a bit of land and the outbuildings of course. I don't know about father's love of keeping sheep but there are other things. In fact, Joe Cordingly is thinking of selling the milk round and dad may buy that if Joe's son decides against it."

"Genna! We could be neighbours - marvellous."

"Perhaps not for long, you could be in Scotland and for me, the big thing is I won't be needed at home any more. I could go on to further education and get qualifications if I sit some exams. I don't know exactly what." Genna went on to ask about Issy's father and it appeared he was making a steady recovery.

"At least the meningitis scare seems to have faded away. How's William in the midst of all this?" Genna's enquiry was casual.

"Yes, thank God, there are no more cases. I think Wills regards the rest as a big intrusion - not your family stuff, just the media thing."

"Of course. How are thing going with John?"

"He complains he couldn't turn his back for two minutes without me getting up to something and why hadn't I told him about it? I did keep asking him about 'The Croft' but everything was sidetracked with this blessed pot. That's the big news - the plaster coming off."

"Brilliant. There'll be no holding you."

"I'll have to think more carefully about what I'm doing. Listen, why don't you come up here for an hour or two this afternoon. It's going to be really warm. We can sit in the garden. You deserve a break."

Genna paused, she would have liked nothing better but it might result in her bumping into William and she was not sure if she wanted to do that. She told herself not to be ridiculous. She could not go on avoiding William for ever. Better get it over with.

When Genna arrived Issy was in a secluded corner of 'The Rectory' garden, not quite in the shade of an old beach from where the murmur of voices could be heard as people drifted up the lane. She was lying full length, resplendent in a spotted bikini, one foot gently pushing off from the ground making the swinging sun lounger rock gently.

"Hi, Issy, I like the one white and one brown." Genna pointed to Issy's legs as she collapsed into the chair obviously waiting for her.

"I am trying very hard to get them even. I feel daft with one white leg but at least they say I am healing nicely and I have just to be careful. But, Genna, I'm so pleased you've come. I'm bored to tears with all this sunbathing. There's a bikini for you there if you want to soak it up while we talk and there's some sun block."

Genna slipped out of her clothes and into the bikini. Her skin was smooth and brown already as she often worked outside wearing next to nothing.

Issy had to be congratulated on her thoughtfulness. Maybe the idea of Scotland and isolation was beginning to hit home. A white garden table with a large glass jug of orange juice with fruit and ice stood alongside tall glasses.

Fifi was stretched out on the grass beside Issy. The dog was peaceful. Genna wondered how she would cope with the wilds of Scotland. She lay back in the sun chair with the icy glass in her hand, feeling guilty that she was so idle.

"Do you think you and Fifi will like it amongst the banks and braes?"

"I cannot think of a better place to be. There's a popular phrase to describe how I feel about John at the present time; I could shag him to bits and not much else matters."

Genna spluttered into her drink laughing, it was so typical of Issy, live for the moment and jigger the rest.

The peace of the afternoon was disturbed by the crunch of tyres on the gravel behind the laurel hedge. Both girls and dog sat up. Fifi barked furiously, head up, back legs splayed out. Issy grabbed for her wrap over blue sun dress which was draped over the back of the seat "I expect it could be John but he's early."

Genna's heart was banging in case it was somebody else. Fifi's tail began to waggle and she found she was right. William's head appeared round the laurel hedge. Fifi dashed towards him ecstatically and William bent down to greet her. Issy threw down the sundress as he made for the orange juice like a camel with a thirst, undoing his tie and loosening his shirt as he walked.

"Don't worry girls I won't spoil your garden party. I can tell you father's doing fine and I just saw John. He said to tell you he would come as soon as he could but he went into the office and there's a job to see to." He poured orange juice and ice into a glass. "Cheers!" He toasted the pair looking in Genna's direction. "Genna I feel in awe at meeting such a celebrity."

"Hardly that... I really didn't do much to deserve that status." Genna managed without her voice shaking.

"You and Issy have certainly stirred up some dust

at 'The Croft'"

"Rather profitable dust as far as Genna is concerned." Issy was unaware of the tension between the two."

"So it would seem." William sounded depressed and tired all of a sudden. Genna wanted to go over to him and tell him everything would be alright He took a long drink of the orange juice. "Congratulations, anyway on all the implications of your find. I hope it all goes in the right direction." He lifted his glass to her.

"I'm really glad your dad's okay. Has the meningitis scare calmed down.?"

"Nothing to report at the moment. We're keeping our fingers crossed. Actually your foray into the past has taken the pressure off. People forget quickly and go on to the next thing." He pushed blond hair off his forehead so that the dark shadows under his eyes were more obvious. "Everybody's scampering up to 'The Croft' since the newspapers took over."

His words echoed in Genna's mind, 'forget and go onto the next thing'.

"When are you starting the diet, Isso?" He almost smiled, Genna noted.

"If you can't be complimentary, don't bother." Issy growled back.

"There are worse things to bear. I've just been dealing with one."

"I hope it's nobody I know." Issy murmured from the depths of the lounger. "Father collapsing's been enough for one week."

"In a way. Do you remember the owner of the tea shop"

"Of course, you mean Bessie?"

"She died this morning."

"Oh no! "Genna looked at him aghast. "I didn't even know she was ill."

"Not one for talking about her troubles, Bess. She had a slow growing brain tumour for some time. We were managing to treat it conservatively without an op. But a few days ago she had a stroke and died in Kettlington Hospital this morning. I've never seen a family so devastated. They were a very close bunch."

"What a rotten shame. "Genna shook her head disbelievingly. She thought of Bess in her constant headscarf and her advice about enjoying life while you could. Issy was right. "Live happily today, tomorrow could be too late. That should be put on her grave," she murmured half to herself.

"Too true. But as my sister's favourite idea goes, 'If there's no time to kiss the cat and walk round the table, you can't stop to think about being happy.' Are you in the pub tonight, Genna? I may drop by after we've eaten."

"I wouldn't bother."

"Why's that?"

"The Harley Davison gang are camping not far away and the place will be full of motorbikes and black leathers, so Pete told me earlier and by the way, he asked me to apologies for the other night."

William frowned in reply as he remembered.

"William... WILLIAM ... telephone." The conversation was halted as Marjorie's voice drifted across the garden from the house. William heaved himself out of the chair with a groan.

"Hell's teeth! I wouldn't be surprised if they called me to the phone when I'm nailed down in my coffin. By the way, don't bother to slim, Isso," he called over his shoulder. I'm sure John will be pretty happy with you the way thing are - odd legs and all the rest!"

"What was that all about, Genna - apologies from Pete? "

"Oh, nothing, they had their wires crossed a bit." Genna brushed it off, sounding bored and realised she was getting as good as Issy in evading the truth.

It was as Pete had foreseen, the pub was a seething mass of bikers dressed mostly in black leather and with gleaming immaculate machines displayed on the cobbles outside. The riders were older enthusiasts; Pete said they were often professional people. 'The Unicorn' was always glad to entertain them. They drank beer, camped on the moors over the weekend and rarely made trouble.

Pete had engaged a new girl, a slant eyed blonde to help with the bar and Genna could see his attentions had been diverted in that direction so she had no need to be apprehensive about him breaking his promise.

Through the atmosphere in the pub Genna never saw William at the door peering through the haze of talk and laughter, trying to catch her eye. He turned and walked away, knowing it would be of no use trying to exchange even brief words with her.

Genna collapsed into bed about midnight. Thunder clouds had crept up later in the evening and as she put her head on the pillow she heard rain starting to pound on the roof. Heavy rain. The water levels were still high and even though the day had been warm the rivers were nevertheless well up their banks.

The days had sped by like a logging rive in full flow with herself the lumbar jack jumping from one fast moving tree trunk to another. She reached out to turn off the small bedside light, hoping sleep would come more easily than it had done in the past few nights.

She awoke in the early hours to an almighty bang after lightning split the darkness and more rain pelted down outside. They would have to start looking for the leaks tomorrow if this continued.

Sunday dawned although it was not easy to detect.. Mist and cloud surged slowly around the heights of the Dales, torturing and twisting the shapes of the hills as rain fell steadily. Sheep huddled under walls trying to stay out of the wet. The light grew stronger and it seemed that humanity had deserted the Elvingdale scene and gone to ground in dry houses with doors and windows tightly shut.

Eddy Mcfaiden came in for breakfast about 9:30 am. looking pleased to be back in the warm kitchen. He had been moving stock from the lower fields down by the river.

Genna was cooking bacon and eggs as he stripped off an old dripping Mackintosh and a bedraggled cap that had the texture of a soggy Yorkshire pudding. "Alright Dad?"

"Aye, I reckon so. Maybe there won't be a chance to do much more of this."

"You mean you'll really miss it?"

"Could be. I've done it all my life. Dare say I shan't in the winter but it's full of life out there this morning...surging with energy. At that moment Jose came through the yard door and placed a basked of fresh eggs carefully on the kitchen table after propping a wet umbrella on the stone sink.

"Ed, I was just thinking, the last time there was rain like this in early summer some lambs wandered over to the island when the stream was calmer, you know down below the mid-fell fields. When the water came down from the hills the stream flooded suddenly and they were cut off, nearly swept away and drowned."

"I remember well enough. Nobody saw it coming, You made a good job saving them and you're thinking it could happen again?"

"Don't know but we'd best check."

Eddy regarded the full plate of in front of him,

obviously trying to decide whether the lambs were going to survive for ten minutes while he ate his bacon and eggs. "I'll just finish this and go."

"No, Dad, don't worry," Genna chipped in, "I'll take the truck up the road and drive down the cart track. I'll manage okay."

Eddy paused, looking at his daughter. "Alright, but stay on the track, mind you. Don't go onto the soft ground."

"Will do." Genna called back as she went to collect her Wellington and rain gear, at the same time pulling on an old wide brimmed hat before she started to head on into the downpour outside.

"Don't be trying any heroics. If there are difficulties come straight back." Her father's voice followed her out of the door.

Getting the truck down the car track into the field had been no problem. She saw how her mother had been right. Walking the distance to the swollen stream in the bottom she heard the bleat of young lambs before she saw them. As she drew closer she spotted a few youngsters stranded on the small island where the grass was sweet. The lambs were not small or weak, in fact they looked quite sturdy but they were scared and stuck, bleating to the ewes standing on the banks.

The torrent of water which had once been a stream, seemed to be rising all the time as the rain lashed down and the island grew smaller.

It proved to be far from an easy task half carrying and half helping the now heavy lambs to safety.

She realised before wading into the water, her Macintosh was going to be in the way and she had taken it off and thrown it sodden into the back of the truck. The water swirled and gushed, fighting to get over the top of her Wellingtons and partially succeeding.

At last all the families were reunited and Genna collapsed, soaked and breathless onto the driving seat of the truck. Having done so she then realised it would be better to put the lambs into the back of the truck in case they were daft enough to go back and tangle with the stream again. She knew if she drove off the ewes would follow. She clambered out into the rain once more.

The task completed, she thanked her foresight that she had already turned the truck around so that it was ready to go up the hill track. She started the engine and eased it gently forward. As fate would have it one wheel came to rest on a soft patch of ground and as soon as she revved even gently to go forward the wheel sank down into the mud leaving the truck at a tilt. She cursed her stupidity. Now she would have to think of a way to coax it.

The engine stalled a couple of times and she got out, shirt clinging to her skin. She could not help thinking what a good entry she would make for a wet vest competition wearing no bra and her nipples hard, sticking to the thin material. She looked for sacking in the back of the truck; pushed flat under the wheel it should give some grip.

The sacking in place and her hands wet and scraped, she returned to the driving seat and tried once more, pushing wet strands of hair off her face so that she could see.

The engine was flat, not a squeak in it. She sat there looking out at the rain, feeling dejected and miserable, defeated all round. She pulled herself up sharply. What on earth was the matter with her? This was no way to be. She was within a hair's breadth of freedom, a new life with education and career prospects, everything she had always wished for, yet all she could do was just sit there and feel sorry for herself because of a bucket or two or water and a duff truck.

She pulled off the wide brimmed hat, shook it and stuffed it back on her head. Getting out, she made sure the lambs were safe and headed for the walk up the hill towards the road. Her gaze faltered as she saw a figure walking towards her.

She watched, stopping in her tracks to see who it was. Her heart seemed to turn over as she recognised William. Had he come to look for her? Was her mother ill? She set off clumsily towards him, the soggy Wellingtons slipping and skidding as the cart track turned to mud with the water running down it. The rain was getting in her eyes but she could see William sliding and skidding down the hill, smiling as though he could not wait another minute.

For Genna the clouds may well have cleared, pushed as though by a large invisible hand to uncover the sun streaming with a golden light from its heights onto the green fields below. Emily Gatenby's phrase ran into her mind 'a flight of the emotions to a sun filled heaven', such was the elation that overtook her as she saw William eager to reach her.

Her thoughts skipped over each other, tumbling through the last few days; the stark unhappiness she had learned of in the life of her grandmother, was not the least of them. She knew now what had made her feel so wretched and despairing.

"Genna!" William grabbed her hand, "I CANNOT do this casual stuff. If it's what you wanted, I'm sorry but for me it's a proper relationship or nothing."

She nodded and he grabbed her towards him urgently and regardless that they may both have been standing under a waterfall. He kissed her wet face eyes and mouth then looked down at her shirt, his eyes crinkling in delight at the sight before him. His happiness was obvious and the fact that he had no reservations about wanting her.

As for Genna, the feeling that overcame her in his presence and the fact he had come to seek her out, wiped out all the uncertainty she had experienced over the last few days. If this was pure happiness then all the happy people in the world must feel like shouting to heaven as she did, a shout to awake the dead and tell Emily Gatenby that her loss and long misery had come right in the end for her own granddaughter. Education she would find but somewhere William had to come into the scheme of things permanently in her life

She took a gasp of air after the climbing and the kissing and looked up at him, her hat tilted to the back of her head as he spoke.

"I called at the farm and your father said…"

"I knew it all along" she smiled, "it's my money you're after."

"Oh sure! You can keep your money all to yourself," he smiled back. "Give it away if you want." He shook her shoulders gently. "It's time you started taking me seriously. I don't want any more shadowy, unreliable women. You are the real thing. I love you and I need you beside me. Can you cope with that? If you can, we'll organise something properly for ourselves."

Genna laughed up at him with joy at his intensity and the manner of his proposal. Issy had always said there was more to him that he allowed the world to see. "William, I can cope with that; I have always loved you to distraction, ever since I dropped the cake on the floor but if we are going to be real, I'm soaked to my knickers and I have a cart load of sheep down there. Can we organise that first?"

William smiled back at her silently applauding her realism.

They turned in the rain, his arm around her shoulder, two small figures framed against the grandeur of the hills as they made for the truck and its bleating lambs.

53653072R00175

Made in the USA
Charleston, SC
15 March 2016